AN UNFAMILIAR LANDSCAPE

Amanda Huggins is the author of the novellas *All Our Squandered Beauty* and *Crossing the Lines*, as well as four previous collections of short fiction and poetry. She was a runner-up in the Costa Short Story Award 2018 and her prize-winning story 'Red' features in her collection *Scratched Enamel Heart*. In 2020 she won the Colm Toibin International Short Story Award, was included in the BIFFY50 list of Best British and Irish Flash Fiction 2019–20, and her poetry chapbook, *The Collective Nouns for Birds*, won the Saboteur Award for Best Poetry Pamphlet. In 2021 *All Our Squandered Beauty* won the Saboteur Award for Best Novella and Amanda also won the H E Bates Short Story Competition and was Highly Commended in the Fish Short Story Prize. She grew up on the North Yorkshire coast, moved to London in the 1990s, and now lives in West Yorkshire.

An Unfamiliar Landscape

Amanda Huggins

Valley Press

First published in 2022 by Valley Press
Woodend, The Crescent, Scarborough, YO11 2PW
www.valleypressuk.com

ISBN 978-1-912436-82-8
Cat. no. VP0199

A CIP record for this book is available from the British Library.

Cover and text design by Peter Barnfather.
Cover art: *Tokyo Ghost* (2021) by Suzanne Conboy-Hill.
Edited by Teika Bellamy.

Printed and bound in Great Britain
by TJ Books Limited

For everyone who has walked through the dark wood,
especially those who have yet to come out the other side.

Contents

Aleksandr

I watch Alex through the kitchen window. He turns his collar up against the salt-licked wind, walks past without looking up, his wool cap pulled low.

The room is quiet and hollow now he's gone, the mantel clock widening the emptiness as it strikes the hour. Alex said it would be fine, my mother taking the baby for a few days, he said it would do me good to have a break. But I miss the wee boy already, the straightforward way he fills each day with the mundane, the way he tangles me up in his needs, sweeps me up with his smile. He shows me the best of myself, leaves no room for the dark doubt underneath.

I say my husband's name out loud. Aleksandr. I try to pronounce it the way his mother does, turning it over in my mouth. The sharp bite of the 'k' followed by the soft hiss of the 's', then the sigh of the fall and the short uptick of the finish.

Aleksandr, Aleksandr, Aleksandr.

When I first met him – first craved him – I thrilled to hear his mother say it, pronouncing it in her beautiful Russian accent. The anticipation made me dizzy. I mouthed 'Aleksandr' at my reflection in the mirror, conscious of the way the word was formed by my lips, my tongue, my teeth. It raced down my spine in a way I knew it never would again after the first time we made love. His name was a precious gift, a gift I still hold tightly to my ribs, never daring to call him it for fear it will shatter. To everyone other than his mother he is always Alex.

I stack the bowls and plates on the shelf, turn back to the window, pause for a moment when I see him in the distance outside the herring shed. I clutch the edge of the sink until the door swings shut behind him, then I let go of my breath, watch it curl around the room like sea mist.

If Alex were to get his job back on the trawlers then perhaps he would walk tall again, north wind or no wind, no longer cowed by the weight of his needless guilt. It follows him around the house, a monkey clinging to his back, and when he leaves for work he carries it with him in his knapsack. At night it lies between us in the bed, and he turns away from it, scratches his arms as though he can feel its fingers tapping.

He says he only wants the best for me, for our baby, and I tell him we already have the best. I chose this life. I always understood it would be hard, realised that new clothes and expensive dinners would be rare. I'd seen the damp patches on the parlour walls, knew I would be dragging buckets of coal from the cellar and struggling to keep the Aga alight, that I would be fighting the rain and the wind to carry washing out to the scullery in the winter. This is exactly the life I expected when I made my choice, and it's a good life, an honest life, a solid life.

But this morning I'm temporarily uprooted, drifting, trying to float above the high wall that bricks me in a little further every day. My comforting mantra no longer rings true; I'm unsure that anything can make Alex walk tall again.

At ten o'clock I shrug on my parka, fetch my purse, count out the last of my coins. I open the cupboards and the fridge one last time, consider what I can make with two tins of tomatoes and half a bag of potatoes, wonder if I dare ask for more credit at the village shop.

As I close the fridge door, I see a flash of crimson through the window. A stout woman clutching a beribboned box picks her way across the muddy lane, holds her coat with her free hand to avoid it snagging on the lobster pots by the gate.

I pull the door open, feel the edge catching against the swollen frame.

'Aunt Florence, what a lovely surprise! Come in, come in, you must be frozen in that thin coat.'

I slip off my parka, pull a chair across the flags towards the Aga, throw a cushion down. I busy myself with the teapot, rinse it with hot water, spoon in the tea.

'Stanley wanted a drive out, Yorkshire weather or not. We were feeling like two sailors with cabin fever. So I said we might as well come over to visit my lovely nephew and bring the boy's belated christening gift.'

'Where's Stanley now?'

'Oh, he decided to stay in the car. We're parked just around the back. There's some programme on the radio he wants to listen to. Where is my Alex today anyway?'

'He's doing a shift down at the herring sheds.'

'I could pop down and see him for a moment.'

'I don't think you'd better. His boss is...' I trail off, hear Florence sniff as she looks away and glances around the room, taking in the worn rag rug, the clothes drying on the rack. A large silk-covered box sits on the table between us, rain-spotted, yet unmistakably luxurious. Florence makes sure it has pride of place in the centre, pushing aside the wooden butter bowl filled with my painted eggs. Nevertheless, the eggs catch her eye and she picks one up to examine it.

'Careful, they're...'

Before I can finish my sentence the eggshell dents under the pressure of her thumb. She drops it quickly back into the bowl.

'Sorry, Lindy, but how was I to know? I thought they were wood or something.'

'It's okay,' I say, but we both know it isn't.

'Where is the boy?' she asks, changing the subject, gesturing around the room as though she expects my baby to be hidden in one of the cupboards.

I'm still looking at the broken egg, wondering if I can repair it somehow. I press my hands to my knees beneath the check cloth, try to stop myself from reaching out for it. It's my favourite egg, the one depicting the girl with yellow flowers in her hair and the boy with the bright blue eyes.

'My mother has him for a few days. She's taking him to visit my Aunt Noosh.'

'Oh, such a shame! I wanted to see the child's face when you open his gift. But you can look anyway.'

Florence picks up the box and hands it to me. I thank her, my heart already heavy. I can see it's from an expensive jeweller's in Harrogate, and I know the gift will be unsuitable, that it won't enrich my baby's life or fix the gable end where the rain drives through.

A gold christening bangle rests on blue velvet. I stare at it, take in the gleam and shine, but I don't touch it.

'It's beautiful. Thank you so much.'

Florence reaches across, takes it from the box and holds it up to the light.

'It's a boy's – look, it's much chunkier than the ones meant for girls. Apparently they're all the rage now. Solid gold as well. An investment.'

I hear myself swallow. 'Thank you, Aunt Florence, I'm sure he'll treasure it.'

'Oh it's nothing! Only the best for my great-nephew.'

After Florence leaves, I pick up my coat again, slip the christening bangle into the inside pocket. As I cross to the door I see Alex through the window, a tiny figure by the slipway. He picks up a wooden crate and goes back inside the shed.

There is something apologetic about the way he stands and moves, the way he hunches down as though he's trying to take up less space in the world. I know he hates being on land, that he feels tied to the sea by an invisible thread, that it pulls him back with every ebbing tide.

I remember him telling me about the herring sheds when we first met; he was proud of his skills on the splitter, the skills his father taught him so well when he was still at school. But I know he never thought he'd have to work there.

Derek Machin came by the cottage after what happened on the trawler. I didn't tell Alex he'd called, and he won't be pleased if he ever finds out I begged for his job.

'I can't take him back on the *Sally Ann*, Lindy, I just can't. He's a danger to my crew when his anger flares up like that. The lad has no self-control. Terry would have gone overboard if it hadn't been for Pete's quick reaction. I might have reconsidered, but when I asked him to apologise, he refused.'

I nodded as though I understood, but I still don't know for certain what happened out there. Did the boy who saw us in the dunes tell everyone in the village? I only found out later he was Terry's son. Did Terry tease Alex about it until he lost his temper?

It had been as dark as sea coal that night, but when the clouds parted for a moment, a bright moon flooded the beach. I never told Alex about the boy who was watching us. When I saw his head appear over the top of the dunes I said nothing. I allowed him to watch me sitting astride Alex, my skin milk-pale in the silver light, my hair loose down my back. I performed for him, emboldened, mermaid-slick, until the clouds raced across the moon again.

In the beginning we made love wherever and whenever we wanted: in the dark woodland, cushioned by a bed of leaves; on the firm sand at the shoreline, our cries muffled by the crash of the receding waves; up on the open moorland beneath wide gold skies. We were tireless, greedy for the taste of each other. Alex picked me flowers then – anemones and primroses in the spring, wild roses in the summer. He gave me handfuls of rumbled sea glass which I still keep in a chipped glass jar on the window ledge. And when I stained my favourite grey boots with coal dust, he painted patterns on the leather to hide the marks, added birds and ribbons, hearts and anchors.

Each spring, before my birthday, Alex stole an egg from Johnny Carter's henhouse. He crept across their yard in the early light, and I imagined the egg cupped gently in his hand, cool as stone, as he climbed back over the fence. After the first time, I told him he could take one of ours from the pantry shelf, but he said it wouldn't truly be a gift if he did it that way. He carried the egg straight down to the boathouse, and when he'd blown it clean he painted it with the enamel paints he kept there. Every year he copied a traditional Russian design from his mother's book: scenes of troikas and domed churches, country dachas, dashing Cossacks and rosy-cheeked girls with plaits wound around their heads. Then he placed the decorated egg in a nest of straw and left it on the bedside chair while I was still sleeping.

This year my birthday fell just after the boy was born, and for the first time there was no egg waiting for me on the chair when I woke up. Instead, there was an expensive box of violet creams from some exclusive London store, delivered at great expense.

Those early gifts, those things from the sea and the land, were – are – everything I could ever want, yet now Alex's guilt buys me things I resent. He tells me I deserve the best, yet he can't see he's giving me much less. The extravagant bouquets from the florist, the handmade baby shoes, the silk slip embroidered with lilies. Yet the electricity bill is always paid on the last demand, the coal merchant threatens to refuse credit, and on the rare occasion when a bill is settled on time it's always Alex's slate at the Pig and Anchor.

He tells me he'll stop drinking soon; he will, he will, he will. But he needs it now – just once a week, or maybe twice. He traces a finger down my cheek, says he can't face the sad beauty in my face, the knowledge that he's let me down – is letting me down – day after day. I lie and tell him he isn't, yet my reassurances don't sound as solid as they did before the baby came.

I pull on my old boots. The patterns Alex painted are faded and covered by new stains now, the soles starting to peel away at the toes. I step carefully around the deeper puddles, tap on Marie Merriweather's door, look around to make sure no one is watching.

Marie's eyes glint when she sees the bangle. 'I can offer you a set price now, or you can leave it with me to see how much Billy can sell it for – usual terms. You takes your chance as always.'

I remember the coins in my purse, the empty cupboard, and I know there isn't enough coal for tonight. 'What can you offer me now?'

Marie sucks in her cheeks, pushes her glasses down her nose and pretends to examine the hallmark.

'I have the original box back at home if you need it.'

'£35.'

'£45?'

'£40 is the most I can give you now. Or you can wait, like I said.'

She reaches forward impulsively, rests her fingers on my wrist. 'This needs to be sorted out, Lindy. You and Alex can't go on like this, just because of what Terry's son saw.'

So it was as I thought. I snatch my hand back and shake my head.

'I'll fetch the box. Don't ever tell anyone where you got the bracelet, not even Billy. I can't have Alex knowing I ever had it.'

I build a good fire, make a casserole, pour two glasses of cheap red wine. At ten o'clock Alex isn't home. Sometimes he helps to mend nets and pots after his shift, or does odd jobs for Alan at the main boathouse. But he didn't say he'd be late tonight.

I kick the coal scuttle when I realise my stupidity. It's Friday. He'll be in the Pig and Anchor, counting out the money he always keeps back: the odd fiver, some loose change, tucked inside the pockets of the old coat hanging on the door. And even if there is no money there, even if I've already taken it for groceries, he always wangles credit.

I should never have gone over to Marie's today. Not on a Friday. Billy Merriweather is sure to be in the Anchor right now.

I can hear his voice.

'Pay day, Alex?'

Alex will turn to see Billy at his shoulder, holding something beneath the bar, palmed in his left hand.

'I've got just the thing for you,' he'll say softly. 'Just the thing to make it right with the little lady when you get home after three too many. This'll soft-soap her – something for the wee lad.'

He'll see the glint of it as Billy lifts his arm.

'I have the box for it too – dead smart.'

Alex will turn it around in his hand, feel the weight of it, as heavy as his heart.

'How much?'

'£100. It's a bargain. £170 plus it would cost yer in the jeweller's.'

'I don't get paid again until next week.'

Then he'll think about the way my face lights up when I smile, the boy's face as he sleeps. '£80? £40 next week, £40 the fortnight after that, but I get to take it home today. You know I'm good for it.'

Alex will cradle the box in both hands as he walks up to the cottage. He'll tell himself it will make me happy and believe it to be true. Why shouldn't we have it, he'll ask? Only the best for our baby.

I stand up and open the door when I hear the gate creak.

'I can't wait to see your face when you open this box,' he says.

'Have you been in the Anchor?' I ask.

'Just for one, earlier,' he says. 'I've been doing some work in the boathouse tonight.'

'Was Billy in the pub?'

Alex nods. 'He gave me some good advice as it happens; a bit of a talking to if I'm honest.' He shakes his head and smiles to himself.

I hardly listen to him. I can see it's the same box, the slub silk still spotted with marks from the earlier rain, the ribbon now missing.

He places it on the table. 'Go on,' he says, smiling.

My hand shakes a little as I lift the lid. There is a nest of straw inside, dry wisps of it fall onto the check cloth. His gift sits in the centre, liquid gold in the firelight. I pick it up carefully, this thing so hopelessly weak and yet so extraordinarily strong. The detail is exquisite: a man and a woman stand in front of a small house, lamplight shining out through the windows, a baby held in the crook of the woman's arm. The rest of the egg is washed in gold.

He laughs at the wonder in my face.

'I'm so sorry, Lindy,' he says. 'For all of it. I'll make everything right.' He rummages in his pocket and then holds up the bangle.

'What? I—'

'Ssh, I've sorted it out, don't worry.'

He pulls me to him and I can feel the rough callous on his right palm as he reaches for my hand, smell the salt-dark of him, a trace of woodsmoke, see the neatly stitched tear in his coat near the shoulder seam.

'Aleksandr,' I whisper, and I feel his name running down my spine.

The Sparrow Steps

How often did you recall that last afternoon in Haradani-en garden? I can still remember the clear blue skies, hear the leaves crackle underfoot. I held out the dry skeleton of a cherry leaf, told you autumn was proof that death could be beautiful. You took it from me, twisting the stem between your fingers.

'So fragile,' you said.

You lagged behind as we climbed the hill, and when we reached the top you paused, out of breath. I laughed, said we were getting older, but you didn't reply. I think you hoped your silence would go unnoticed, yet I could hear every word you'd bitten back ringing out down the hillside and echoing around Kinkaku-ji temple.

We stopped at a bridge on the way back, and you sat on the steps to unfasten your boot, removed a small stone that was pressing into your heel. I crouched beside you, watched as you ran your fingertips over a row of bird footprints, captured forever in the newly laid concrete.

'Proof we can sometimes leave an eternal mark, that we live on after our beautiful deaths,' you said.

I took a photograph of the prints next to your splayed hand; the immortal footsteps of sparrows, like tiny dinosaur fossils.

'We should make a pledge,' I said. 'A vow that if we ever lose touch we'll meet here at the sparrow steps ten years from today?'

I was so sure we'd never be apart. It was an easy promise.

You looked up at the cherry trees, and for a moment I remembered them in spring: petals delicate as insect wings, fluttering down like a whisper of moths, the trees bowing with the weight of their fleeting beauty.

That's when I saw the uncertainty in your eyes.

'Yes,' you said, quietly. 'We should do that.'

Eating Unobserved

The letting agent urged Marnie to admire the handmade kitchen cabinets, to appreciate the proportions of the bedroom fireplace. But there was really no need. She'd decided to take the apartment on Rue Annette as soon as she walked into the salon, captivated by the high ceilings, the elaborate cornice, the flood of light from the huge windows. They were almost as tall as the room itself, still fitted with the original sun-faded shutters.

The concierge apologised for the furniture. He said it had been left by the previous tenant, a Madame Hubert. She'd moved abroad quite suddenly and he hadn't had time to clear the rooms. Yet Marnie loved the worn chaise longue, the crystal chandelier in the hallway, the pale grey bedstead decorated with overblown roses. The walls were filled with foxed watercolours, pen and ink sketches of Parisian streets, portraits of forgotten ancestors. She told the concierge he could leave it all just as it was.

And in the bedroom there was a glorious oil painting, depicting a sumptuous banquet – a sensual feast of fruit, cheeses, fish and game, spilling out across a thick linen cloth. Figs were split wide open, ripe and glistening; succulent peaches wore a velvet bloom, tempting the observer to bite into their yielding flesh, to lap up the sticky spill of warm juice. Fish lay on blue platters, mouths agape, their scales glittering and slippery; rich, silky cheeses collided, their melting centres running over the edge of the board.

And when Marnie lay in bed, gazing at the painting,

something inside her melted with them.

The day after she moved in, she dragged the heavy dining table across to the windows, decided she would work there in the daytime and eat her dinner there every evening. It was late autumn, too cool to eat outside on the narrow balcony, but the windows faced east, caught the sunlight during the mornings, and she could imagine how it would be in the spring. She'd buy a simple gingham cloth, enjoy breakfasts of flaky croissants and warm baguettes, brew freshly ground coffee, crowd the table with tiny dishes filled with curls of pale unsalted butter, apricot jam, fig preserve, lavender honey.

And in the evenings she might take her dinner at the small bistro on the corner. She would order simple, straightforward dishes: steak, mussels, a seasonal omelette, bread with a thick floured crust, a carafe of house wine.

But all that was for the future, when the advance came through for her next book – the novel she'd given herself six months in Paris to finish. For now she would be disciplined, work in the apartment most of the time, occasionally venturing out to cafés with her notebook, and she'd eat her dinners alone at home.

Marnie fell into an effortless routine. She bought fish and vegetables from the market each morning, bouquets of fresh herbs tied with rough twine. She wrote in the afternoons, and when the light faded she pored over the yellowed pages of the cookery books left behind by Madame Hubert, practised making bouillabaisse, croquettes and crêpes. Every evening she dressed the table as though for an opulent dinner, with candles, flowers, platters of fruit, the embroidered tablecloths and heavy silverware she discovered tucked away at the back of the kitchen press.

And when she went to bed she gazed at the painting of

the banquet, half lit by the streetlamp, and in her dreams she walked into its rich dark heart, was swallowed whole by its slippery, lubricious flesh.

The building directly across the narrow street appeared to be empty, and in the evenings the rooms remained in darkness. Most of the windows were shuttered, save for the second floor apartment she looked down on, which showed signs of recent occupation; it was brightly painted outside, with a striped awning over the salon window and red geraniums in glazed pots. But for the moment, there was no one to watch and nobody watching, and at dusk Marnie lit candles and sat by the window, eating unobserved. She had given herself Paris as a gift, yet now she had unwrapped it she hardly knew what to do with it. Every morning she woke with an unfathomable longing; the half-remembered remnants of a dream slipping away at first light.

Occasionally she heard noises in the rooms above and beneath her own: footsteps pacing back and forth across the parquet floor, a loud cough through an open window, a radio playing. But she never passed anyone on the stairs or in the lobby, and her spoken French wasn't good enough to strike up a conversation in the café or the market.

If she went to the bathroom in the early hours of the morning, she found herself walking across to the window. Occasionally she saw a lone figure staggering home late, or a stray dog intent on a night-time mission.

Then one evening she saw a light across the street.

The apartment with the striped awning was illuminated by a single lamp. Marnie could make out a coat thrown across a velvet couch, a coffee table piled with books, a flicker of blue light from the television in the corner. A man entered the room and placed a glass of wine on the table. He sat down, stretched out his legs and crossed them at the ankle.

Marnie continued to stand by the window in the dark, strangely compelled by him, by the unknown story, the possibilities, of this stranger's life. When he reached for a pack of Gitanes and she saw the cigarette between his full lips, watched him lean back, inhale deeply, blow his smoke towards the ceiling, she felt the rush of the drug, the pull of the ritual. She went into the bedroom to fetch the Marlboro Lights she'd bought on impulse from a kiosk in the square. They'd remained untouched for three weeks now. She'd kept telling herself it would be stupid to start again after so long, that she didn't want to smoke alone. But tonight she had company.

She walked back into the salon, opened the window to let in the cool air, sat down at the table and pulled out a cigarette. For a few moments it was benign, an unarmed weapon. Then she slipped it between her lips, flicked open the lighter, leaned forward into the small, pale flame, and inhaled.

As she exhaled she looked across the street and realised the apartment opposite was in darkness again.

The following evening, her neighbour arrived home at dusk. Marnie was standing at the window, and she watched him disappear into the building carrying two paper sacks filled with groceries. After a couple of minutes, the kitchen light came on, casting a pool of soft yellow onto a scrubbed farmhouse table. Cupboard doors opened and closed as he packed away tins and packets. He arranged vegetables in a huge earthenware bowl: fat courgettes; green and red peppers; an aubergine, dense, shiny and perfectly smooth; golden onions; overripe tomatoes. Then a cool light shone out from the open refrigerator, spotlighting him as he put away cream and butter, cheeses and saucisson. When the table was finally cleared, he reached for a bottle on a high shelf and poured himself a glass of red wine before starting to cook his supper.

She watched him chop herbs with a mezzaluna before gently whisking three large eggs. When the omelette was ready he cut himself a large hunk of bread and sat down at the table. He ate quickly, with a fierce hunger, his throat pale as he tipped back his head to drink the last of the wine. There was something thrilling and sinful about his beautiful mouth.

She went through to her bedroom and brushed her hair, reapplied her lipstick, changed into her silk robe. It was cold in the unheated room and she shivered a little, then tied the sash tighter before walking back into the salon and flicking on the lamp. She sat down on the chaise longue with her own glass of wine, gazing out into the street.

Tonight she wanted him to see her.

He cleared his supper away and walked into the sitting room, came over to the window and stepped out onto the balcony. He was only a few metres away from her now, and as he fumbled in his pocket for matches, she was tempted to open her own window, to throw her lighter down to him. He appeared to look straight at her, though in the dark it was impossible to tell. For a moment she thought to wave, half-lifted her hand, felt herself smile and blush. But she realised the stupidity of it and dropped her arm, stayed quiet and still, watching him in profile against the light from inside his room, the tip of his cigarette glowing brighter each time he inhaled.

In bed that night, Marnie could hardly concentrate on her book, could only see his strong hands, the fullness of his lips, and when she eventually fell asleep she dreamt he was with her, that they were running together, tiny figures, between towering plates of fruit, biting into black cherries the size of pumpkins, dark juice staining their greedy lips, grabbing handfuls of ripe mango flesh with their bare hands.

From then on, Marnie watched him every evening; she was certain he was watching her too. She would stare, enthralled, as he refilled his wine glass, smoked a cigarette, ate a clementine or a pear, licked the juice from his lips. He would read his newspaper or a book, turn on the television, but every so often he'd look across at her building, his face almost expressionless.

She tried to impress him with new dishes: langoustines, spaghetti vongole, salad niçoise, asparagus risotto. She dressed for dinner, decorated the table with flowers, performed for him as though she were an actor in a one-woman play.

In early December, it snowed. Swirling flakes thudded gently against the windows, reminding her of moths drawn to the light. Marnie sat at the table, watched her neighbour stand up and press his hands to the glass, staring out as though transfixed. Something in his stance emboldened her. She switched off the lamp, untied her robe and let it slip to the floor. She walked over to the window, pressed her own hands to the glass in a mirror pose. He stared out, unblinking, and she found herself unable to move, pinned to the night sky by the falling snow. Yet still his face gave nothing away.

The next day was Saturday, the snow had already melted, and Marnie decided to go down to the market. As she bought her bread, she saw him at the vegetable stall behind her. She blushed, embarrassed, as she remembered her boldness the night before. Yet what did she have to lose now? He was holding up two aubergines, talking to the stall holder in rapid French. She stood at his side, waited for the transaction to be completed.

'Good morning – those are beautiful aubergines,' she said in halting French.

He turned to her, puzzled. 'Do I know you?' he asked in English.

Her blush deepened. 'I live in an apartment opposite your building. I see you sometimes – cooking, smoking on the balcony?'

'So you are spying on me?'

'No!' she gasped. 'Nothing like that! I can see into your room, that's all – when it's dark and you don't close your shutters.'

'I'm sorry, I haven't seen you before.'

'But you must have. You've watched me eating my dinner. And last night...'

She laughed, too embarrassed to say more.

'No, sorry,' he said again, and he shook his head as he walked away.

Marnie followed him home at a distance, wondering why he would pretend not to know her, upset that he would deny having seen her before. As they reached Rue Annette she caught up with him, slipped silently into the lobby behind him as the outer door swung shut. She waited there for a few minutes and then walked up the stairs and knocked on his door.

He answered almost straight away. '*Oui?*'

'I just...' She shrugged, unsure what to say to him now she was there.

He smiled and waved her inside. '*Entrer!* Come in, come in. I apologise – you are my neighbour and I did not mean to be rude. Would you like a coffee, er…?'

'Marnie.'

He shook her hand. 'I am Henri.'

The salon was bright with pale winter sunshine, the table scattered with plates and cups, a wine glass stained red at the rim.

She walked over to the window and gasped. It was impossible to see into her apartment from inside this room. The angle was all wrong, the street so narrow that his awning blocked it out. He would only be able to see into her salon if he were out on the balcony.

As she stood there, a young woman appeared at the window of the apartment beneath her own. Her hair was still sleep-mussed, dark eye make-up smudged. She posed, left hand cupping her right elbow, cigarette held between long fingers. With a rush of embarrassment, Marnie realised that it was this woman, not her, that Henri had been watching from his couch.

'*Voila!*' He set a tray down in a space on the coffee table.

She pointed across to her apartment.

'I live there. The third floor.'

'And as you can see, Marnie, I have no view into your room.'

She nodded. 'I know that now! I thought you were watching me, yet all this time I've been eating alone, unobserved.'

'That's Beatrice,' he said, lifting his hand to acknowledge the woman in the window. 'She works in a bar, so she sleeps late in the mornings. She has two lovers – one for the weekend and one who turns up Monday to Wednesday.'

'So what does she do on Thursdays?'

He laughed. 'She makes sure she gets her story straight.'

Marnie couldn't take her eyes off his mouth as he spoke. His full, soft lips.

'So you are renting Madame Hubert's apartment,' he said. 'Do you know her story?'

She shook her head.

'She was a private tutor, there was a scandal – a young man she taught. They say she seduced him, and his parents attempted to press charges even though he was seventeen. Madame Hubert tried to blame it on a painting in her apartment. She claimed it had sent her crazy with lust! Who would believe that?'

Marnie shook her head again, yet she was barely listening. Her mind was filled with the image of him cutting open a ripe fig, scooping out the dark red flesh with his tongue.

'I have clams,' she said quickly, 'and two bottles of a good white Burgundy – if you'd like to come to dinner tonight?'

He sat down, poured the coffee before he spoke. Their fingers touched as she reached for her cup.

'I will bring dessert,' he said.

Ten of Hearts

I sit on the sofa, you kneel on the floor at my feet. You are charming and eloquent, I am drunk and on the rebound.

'Do you believe in magic?' you ask.

I nod, curious, and you hand me a small sheet of paper from your pocket, tell me to write the name of a playing card in the centre.

You instruct me to fold the paper into a tiny square, then you press it against your forehead, hold it there with a single finger. You ask me to concentrate, to not let it out of my sight. Then you push it inside your clenched fist, drop it back into my palm.

'Your card is the ten of hearts.'

I gasp. How could you possibly know?

You laugh, hold your hands up and lead me to my own bed. 'It's the tenth today,' you say, 'and you've stolen my heart.'

In the morning you kiss me gently before you break the spell, before you explain about sleight of hand and misdirection, how the paper you pressed against your forehead was a blank sheet, folded earlier. You'd already dropped my square to the floor, unfolded it with your free hand under the edge of the sofa; then you read it, refolded it, palmed it, slipped it back into my hand.

You say I'm bound to you forever now, entrusted with one of magic's sacred secrets.

A week later, you move in. We become a double act, performing in every pub for miles around, arriving late when the crowd are unsteady on their feet. Drunken mouths hang agape as lit cigarettes vanish inside your tightly clenched fist never to be seen again. You stake your fake Rolex on a three-card trick, win the punter's confidence and his genuine Omega, produce banknotes from beneath table legs, coins from behind gullible ears. Every time you ask a punter to choose a card they choose the ten of hearts, and you look at me, wink and smile. We steal earrings and bracelets off the earlobes and wrists of the misdirected, slip out into the night with their angry shouts echoing down the street.

You say everything is hotting up, that we need to drive further afield, to sprinkle our magic over a new city. You persuade me to take out a car loan for a shiny new Audi which you register in your name.

Things disappear the night after you collect that gleaming black machine: my watch, my diamond earrings and my debit card, £200 in cash, the lucky ten of hearts I kept safe beneath my pillow. When I challenge you, you act affronted, twisting my words, then carry your suitcases to the car.

When I go over to the window and watch you drive away, I find the ten of hearts Blu-Tacked to the glass. That's when I hear your voice in my head, telling me that magic is nothing more than a set of cheap tricks.

An Unfamiliar Landscape

Is it true that only a suicide stops a Japanese train from running on time?

Why did her father always ask questions about death? In his last letter he'd wanted to know if she knew anyone who had visited Aokigahara, the so-called Suicide Forest. He said he'd read about it in *National Geographic*, that you could sense the spirits when you walked through the trees. And did her husband, Paul, know anyone in his office who had died of *karoshi* – death from overwork?

Sophia pushed the letter back inside her bag, at the same time re-counting the six blister strips of painkillers with her index finger. Reassured by the feel of them, the whisper and rustle of the foil, she snapped the clasp shut and picked up her coffee cup. The café was usually busy, yet that afternoon it was almost empty. For the first time she was aware of the low, slanting light pouring in through the windows, the shoals of yellow leaves in the gutter, and she realised the season had changed without her noticing. Most people were taking advantage of the weather, enjoying the warmth of the October sunshine on their skin.

She drained her cup, stood up to leave, and as she crossed to the door the staff called out their thanks in unison: four ringing voices rising above the hiss of the Synesso machine and the background jazz.

'*Arigato gozaimasu!*'

Sophia still found it impossible to tune out the everyday clamour of Tokyo: the cuckoo signals at pedestrian crossings;

the J-pop and chirpy adverts blaring out from every shop; the cacophonous din of the pachinko parlours; the over-cheerful TV shows with their sherbet-pastel sets. At night, the lights added an extra layer of silent noise; a busy, bright chatter of flashing neon that crowded her head.

She'd been told that even in the villages it was rarely quiet. Her Japanese teacher said piped music and jingles rang out through tannoys in the streets, that the sound carried on the wind to the rice paddies. When she asked why they didn't complain, Fumiko shrugged and said there was nothing to be done. *Shikata ga nai.* It was not to be questioned, it was just part of life.

Sophia had tried to quieten the commotion inside her own head with a daily routine of coffee shops and art galleries, with the hush of museums and books, with endless walks through unfamiliar streets. But inner silence eluded her. She often remembered something her father said when she asked him why he spent so much time in the woods. He told her that solitude was the best companion, that in the wild outdoors it took on a different character, became in itself a connection to the world, an invisible cord between you and your true self.

'I'm alone in the woods,' he'd say, 'but I'm never lonely.'

Sophia called out her thanks and goodbyes as she left the coffee shop, and by the time she reached Yoyogi Park she knew what she must do.

When Paul first announced he'd been offered a transfer to Tokyo, part of Sophia had held back, wanting to say no. Yet it was clear he thought it was the right time to go and that the move would be good for them.

He could no longer face seeing her grief, visible and raw, like an open wound. Yet she knew he'd simply stored away his own, buried it so deep that there were no longer any surface ripples. The loss of a baby wasn't something to "get over", it wasn't a hurdle to leap and leave behind. It was a defining line; a line from which everything would be measured from now on: the time before Calum's death and the time after Calum's death. Grief had already become a part of the warp and weft of her, and at random moments it would rear up unexpectedly with a clatter of hooves. When it did, it was deafening. And unlike the everyday clamour of city life, the noise of grief couldn't be silenced by earplugs or soundproofing.

They flew to Tokyo two weeks before Paul started work, moving straight into the tiny house in Yanesen which had been found for them by Himari, his new assistant. They could have lived in the company apartment block in Roppongi, but Sophia didn't want to be in that part of the city, renowned for its nightlife, its brash expat community. She'd emailed Himari and told her she would rather live somewhere quieter, more traditional.

Himari had picked Yanesen, the area where she herself had grown up, with narrow streets and traditional shops, old wooden houses and a hillside location. A chance to breathe in the city. They were lucky; she found them a house rather than an apartment – albeit tiny. Two traditional *tatami*-floored rooms, one up, one down, with a small kitchen area partitioned off at the back.

They went upstairs and Himari opened the *shoji* screens in the bedroom to show them the enclosed veranda. It overlooked a pocket handkerchief garden of moss and raked gravel, shaded by three small manicured trees. The largest was a mountain cherry. The blossom had already fallen, but Sophia could picture it in full bloom, its pale pink petals newly unfurled. She imagined lying beneath it, looking up at the laden branches and the oblong of perfect blue sky above. The garden was edged by high fencing faced with bamboo screening, and houses similar to their own pressed in around every side. But the outside space, Himari confirmed, was theirs alone.

'I love it,' Sophia said.

For the next two weeks they explored the area, bought new futons and bedding, vintage *kokeshi* dolls from a junk shop, slipware bowls and handmade wooden spoons from the hardware store. Himari suggested they have Western beds delivered, a dining table, but Sophia said no, she was happy with the house as it was: the low table and red floor cushions, the sliding panels decorated with mountain scenes.

The smallest things gave them joy each time they returned home: placing their shoes on the rack in the entranceway, seeing their indoor slippers side by side at the top of the step, inhaling the dusty scent of the *tatami* matting.

On their third weekend in Japan they took a trip to Hakone, arranged by Himari and paid for by the company; a last chance to spend time together before Paul started work.

The bus from the station in Odawara was full of backpackers and sightseers, but as they wound through the main villages and resorts the tourists disembarked, one by one, two by two. The foreign tourists waved maps at the driver, checking and rechecking they were at the right stop, communicating in little more than sign language. As the bus climbed higher, Sophia suddenly noticed the tip of Mount Fuji through the trees. She grabbed Paul's arm, her words tumbling out as she pointed, and the Japanese lady across the aisle beamed with pleasure at her excitement.

'Fuji-san very shy!' she said. 'You are so lucky to see!'

The cloudless sky was cobalt, the snow-capped mountain blue-bright white; a fleeting glimpse of something so beautiful it snatched her breath away. At that moment, Sophia knew it was a sign of luck, could feel it at her core. She sensed a calmness in these trees and mountains, knew she would never feel lonely in this landscape, that there was something essential waiting just beyond her reach. She had uncovered the edgelands of solitude.

After dinner in their room they made love on the *tatami* floor, a red silk kimono spread out beneath them. It wasn't urgent or hurried, like the brief couplings they'd sought to try and block out death; those violent, bruising encounters that felt like bone on bone. It was slow and considered, and it confirmed, without words, that things could be good again.

Yet Sophia's fledgling happiness was short-lived. Paul was required to work long hours, and Sophia was expected to attend dinners with his British and American colleagues.

She found them unbearable. The men were self-important and rude to waiters. Their wives were brittle creatures with helmet hair and heavy jewellery. They spent their days shopping and lunching, and in the evenings they moved their expensive food around on bland restaurant plates and clawed at their husbands' arms with scarlet nails. She was lonely and awkward in their company, out of step, just as she'd been uncomfortable in the London world she'd been pushed into before: champagne-fuelled celebrations in the boardroom accompanied by mutual backslapping, "fun" nights out at the sports bar with unlimited free drinks, Christmas parties at the Café Royal. Her mother always told her she would never fit in, that her Yorkshire accent, her inability to conform, would hold her back.

'They're not your people, Sophia,' she would say.

And her mother had been right. She'd tried in London, for the sake of her career, but here in Tokyo there was no need. Sophia didn't want to fit in – didn't need to fit in – to this sneering world of dismissive expats. She found reasons not to go, until Paul eventually stopped passing on her excuses, and finally she was forgotten.

At first, Sophia enjoyed being alone: the peace of her tiny garden, shopping in the local markets for food, exploring the area. But as the summer went on, she felt suffocated. Even the garden became too hot, the surrounding houses trapping the humid air. The only place to stay cool was in the air-conditioned room downstairs, and she felt hemmed in by its gloom. In Yanesen the shopkeepers and locals were getting to know her, but they didn't speak any English, and their reciprocal bows and smiles, their improvised sign language, could only take her so far.

She asked Paul if Himari could find her a suitable Japanese teacher, and she began to travel across the city to Shibuya three mornings a week to meet with Fumiko.

Fumiko dressed in linen shirts that were the colour of oyster shells and faded sky. She wore a thin gold chain around her neck which caught the light, and her hair was cut in a perfect bob. Sophia coveted its gloss, its inky darkness; she envied Fumiko's quiet containment, her patience with mispronunciations and forgotten vocabulary. Slowly, Sophia moved forward, adding words day by day, words she was sure would reconnect her to the world.

She began by asking Fumiko questions about herself, but her responses were brief and reserved, and when Sophia suggested they went for a coffee one day, she politely declined.

'I am sorry, Sophia-san, it would be very difficult for me,' she said.

In the evenings when Paul came home early she tried to practise her Japanese on him over dinner. But he was always tired and barely listened to her, switching on the portable TV as soon as the dishes were cleared, searching for English language news channels. When she questioned him about work he told her little, and if she called him at the office, Himari would apologise politely and tell her he was too busy to talk.

Sophia was ignored, avoided, silenced, shutdown. She was still disconnected, on the wrong side of an invisible barrier she couldn't push through. Yet the noise of the city and the chatter within her head were both as loud as ever.

Emboldened by her new language skills, she began to explore every area of the city, to take day trips to surrounding towns, to spend time planning journeys to temples and mountains, often returning only at dusk to the house in Yanesen. Her anonymity made her invisible; a ghost moving through the crowds. No one gave her a passing glance on the streets, and in coffee shops and bars, although the staff smiled and nodded excitedly when she ordered in Japanese, they never answered her questions, looked puzzled if she repeated them.

Yet after a few weeks she no longer felt out of place in Tokyo on her own. She knew she could never make the city hers, that she was sliding along its surface and there was no way inside, but it ceased to be important. She explored the streets and parks and galleries, the temples and the teahouses, and every other day, after her class with Fumiko, she drank coffee in her favourite café in Shibuya. As the world strode by the café window, Sophia looked on with calm detachment, and when she was tired of watching she wrote in her journal.

She wrote about their neighbour, Mrs Takahashi, who would knock on Sophia's door and leave a jar of homemade bean jam or a bag of *anpan* buns outside on the step, and about their gardener, Kaito, who appeared every Wednesday morning.

He wore a twill waistcoat covered with pockets, from which he pulled clippers and twine and gloves. Standing on the wooden stepladder he trimmed the small trees with the topiary shears from the storage box, then took the rake and the *shuro* broom from their nails on the wall and combed the gravel, swept away dead leaves. The first time Sophia saw him she went out to talk to him, but Kaito seemed uncomfortable in her presence, and even though she spoke in Japanese he didn't reply. So now she opened the screens before he arrived, then watched him from her chair on the veranda, soothed by his calm, measured movements, by the gentle, rhythmic snips of the cutters, the drag of the rake through the gravel. She sensed his contentment, the beauty and peace of his solitude, and she wished she could feel it too.

She recounted her walks through the city, wrote about the man she glimpsed changing his shirt in a doorway. He revealed a torso that was a riot of fish, flowers, geisha and warriors: the ink badges of a yakuza gangster. He was as colourful as the street fashionistas, but just like the Harajuku girls, his attempt at diversity only reinforced his conformity. And she described the row of shoes – a man's, a woman's, a small girl's – which she saw lined up inside an open doorway. Sophia imagined the family, laughing and talking over dinner, and the daughter, sleepy-eyed, as her mother kissed her goodnight. More than ever, she ached for the life she'd lost, yearned for a new life she barely understood.

She wrote often of her longing for silence, and of how only

suicide prevented a Japanese train from running on time.

She never wrote about Calum: her panic as she'd reached into his cot, her clumsy attempts to revive him, about the guilt and the grief and the never-ending heaviness that pulled at her heart.

She didn't write about the way Paul silenced her as soon as she tried to talk about their son, about how he drank every night after work in the hostess bars and entertained clients in the geisha districts. She didn't mention that she sat on her own in their garden, waiting for him to come home while she listened to the neighbours' chatter and laughter floating down from the open windows.

She didn't write about how sad all of this made her.

Sophia met Akiro one evening when she was walking through the backstreets in Shinjuku. He was taking a cigarette break, standing in the doorway of the Night Owl, when he saw her peering up the steep steps. She was wondering which of the tiny bars to venture into, reading the neon signs that flashed above the doors. He bowed and ushered her upstairs with a sweep of his arm. She ducked her head under a low beam as she went in through the metal door and sat down on the nearest bar stool. She was the only customer.

Akiro told her his name, asked Sophia hers as he placed a clean beer mat and a hot towel on the bar. Then he poured her a beer and lined up two small dishes of rice crackers. She drank the beer too fast, watched a black and white Kurosawa film on the screen behind Akiro's head, listened to the thrum and pulse of music playing through two large speakers as tall as the bar, a tangle of electronic noise and hypnotic whispers that coiled around inside her head. He nodded towards her empty glass and smiled, opened two more bottles of beer, then reached for a bottle of whisky underneath the counter. And around ten o'clock, when no one else had come in, he quietly locked the door.

He stood behind her, reaching around to slide his hand inside her shirt, but as she turned towards him he pulled back, pointing to the back of the bar. She walked in front of him, then stopped, unsure of where they were heading. Akiro pointed to the table and nodded. She understood straight away what he wanted, knew what he needed, knew that she needed it too – a basic human connection, flesh against flesh. No eye contact, no words, no false promises.

Sophia turned away from him, undressed quickly, aware of him behind her as he unfastened his jeans. She gripped the edge of the table without turning round to look at him, arched her back towards him. His breath was warm on the back of her neck as he pressed her forward onto the cool metal surface, and when it was over she realised she was crying.

As she walked to the station through the neon-bright streets, the laughter and chatter of drunken salarymen spilling out from every bar, she understood that all the city could offer her was a different sadness, a constant feeling of jet lag, of disconnection, of things being not quite as they seemed. She was blinded by Tokyo's density. There were no panoramic views, only a set of close-ups at point blank range, the disorientation of an unfamiliar landscape, the knowledge that she was slowly dissolving.

When she arrived home she tiptoed up the stairs, holding her breath, stared at her face in the bathroom mirror as though examining a stranger. She slipped her shirt over her head and noticed how grey her skin appeared in the fluorescent light, how dark her eyes were. She opened the cupboard door and took out the first aid box, reassured herself by counting the boxes of paracetamol. For a while, she had been sure Paul was her saviour, had thought of the pills less and less frequently. But even then they had always been there: a reassurance, a promise of a way out, a talisman perhaps – their presence a lucky charm in itself, their very availability warding off the possibility that she would ever need them.

For the first time since they'd arrived in Tokyo she took out three of the boxes, dropped six blister strips into her bag and pushed the empty packs back into the cupboard with the rest.

She went through to the bedroom and saw straight away the room was empty. As always, she was still alone.

And the following afternoon, as she left the café in Shibuya, she made up her mind to find solitude. She looked up at the trees in Yoyogi Park, the light shining through the red and gold leaves, the long shadows dappling the grass. She knew what she wanted, what she needed to do.

Without telling Paul or leaving a note, Sophia packed a bag and took the train to Matsumoto, then a bus to a village at the foot of the mountains. She walked up the steep hill to the temple lodgings, and they agreed she could take a room for as long as she needed.

The next morning she woke early, collected a map of the walking trails from the temple office and set out before the sun had risen over the higher ridges. She started her ascent through dense forests of larch and beech, following a trail marked by fluttering red ribbons tied haphazardly to branches and rocks. Her footsteps were muffled by fresh leaf fall, and she breathed in the scent of damp, mossy earth. There was a sharp screech from above, a rustle of leaves and cracking twigs as a family of macaques swung overhead.

As she climbed higher she heard distant birdsong and the tap-tap-tap of a pygmy woodpecker. Her heart missed a beat as she crossed a narrow log bridge, gasping at the unexpected drop and the rush and tumble of white water cascading down the rock face. Eventually she cleared the tree line and heard a bear bell tinkle faintly in the distance as a lone climber descended from the highest ridge; a yellow splash against the grey of the rock. Dropped into the silence, every noise had a clear meaning, each sound demanded her attention. She was finally connected.

Later that evening, Michiko, the cook, asked Sophia to walk down to the pond with her to feed the koi. She told her how beautiful it was in the summer when the fireflies came, and of the Japanese belief that the tiny lights were the souls of soldiers who had died in battle.

Sophia thought about the fireflies as she lay on her futon, pictured one of the lights glowing brighter than the rest, imagined it was the departing soul of her own child. As she drifted between waking and sleeping she watched it disappear above the temple and she knew something within her had shifted.

She slept well that night, yet she was awake again at dawn, because as she'd already discovered, the mountains were as full of sound as the city. Outside her room she could hear the dry scrabble of birds' feet in the guttering, the papery whir and flutter of their tiny brown wings. When she walked in the fields she was enveloped in the buzz and rasp and thrum of insects, the rustle of dry grass. At dusk there were the temple bells, the soft lull of the monks' chants, and the gentle clink of pots and pans from the kitchen below her window.

And within this new noise, Sophia finally found her silence.

Lounge Lizards

Art Mainprize is down by the coble landing, perched on the edge of George Cappleman's boat, a crushed beer can ground into the sand below his dangling feet. It's early September, already dark at eight o'clock, and a solemn promise of autumn is wrapped in the cold sea air. When he sees Billy Cappleman heading across from the cottages, he reaches inside the boat and pulls out two more cans. He cracks one open and throws the other to Billy, who catches it awkwardly.

'Thanks.'

'Yer got a light, kidder? I've run out of matches.'

Billy fumbles in the pocket of his Harrington jacket and takes out a cheap disposable lighter. Art pulls a cigarette from a soft pack of Camels and cups his hands around the uncertain flame. He leans back, takes another deep drag and offers the pack to Billy.

'Bit fancy for you, Art? Camels?'

'Da got them off a mate – duty frees from Lloret de Mar or wherever. What's that crap yer wearing anyway?' He pinches Billy's jacket sleeve between his finger and thumb.

'It's what me mam got me from that bloke on the market.'

Art rolls his eyes. 'Bet it's fake then. Don't know what you want it for anyhow. That's what skinheads and Northern soul freaks wear – I thought we were rockers.'

Billy blushes, then shrugs. 'We are. It's just for knocking around down here and stuff. James Dean had one.'

Art scoffs. 'James la-di-da Dean now is it? He yer new role model then?'

‘Nah, not really. Did you know he was bisexual? Like Bowie.’

‘Never heard that before. You seem to know a lot about it? Thinking of trying it out?’

Billy’s blush deepens. ‘Course not.’

Art looks over Billy’s shoulder and lifts his beer can in greeting. ‘Seth – come and have a brown ale. Billy here is just telling me how he’s thinking of going bisexual.’

Seth laughs. ‘That right? I always thought there was summat different about you. What’s that jacket you’re wearing?’

‘There’s nothing wrong with this chuffing jacket. Stop going on about it, the pair of you. There’s far worse sartorial choices made round ’ere. I know someone who wears white slip-on shoes with gold chains across ’em.’

Seth splutters into his beer. ‘What’s “sartorial” mean when it’s at home? And who the bloody hell wears white shoes in this village?’

Billy points at Art. ‘His da, that’s who.’

‘And? So what if he does. My old fella is cool as a Mivvi.’

Billy laughs. ‘My da says men who wear shoes like that are lounge lizards.’

‘Well we don’t have a lounge, so he can’t be.’

‘Ha ha, very funny. Well he wears turtlenecks too, and a cravat, so…’ Billy tails off, knowing he’s probably gone too far.

‘No he bloody doesn’t. You’re just mad because your dad stinks of fish.’

Billy lunges forward and shoves Art in the chest. ‘Better than working in the shite steelworks with a set of losers.’

Brown ale slops out of both beer cans and down the front of Billy’s jacket. Art teeters on the edge of the coble for a second but manages to right himself.

‘The truth always hurts eh, Billy? Shove me like that again

and I might have to tell you something I was hoping to spare you from.'

Art pushes himself off the boat and drops to the ground, starts walking up the slope towards the cottages.

'Wait!' Billy runs after him. 'What do you mean, "something you were hoping to spare me from"?'

Art shakes his head. 'Nothing Billy, nothing, I was just winding you up. I'll see yer tomorrow for the fishing.'

Art lies awake for what feels like hours. There's a full moon shining straight through the thin curtains, and the dog is restless at his feet, her quivering paws running in the air as she sleeps. He feels guilty about what he said to Billy as they parted, knows he'll most probably be wondering about it now. But Art still thinks it would be right to tell him – if he was Billy he'd want to know all the rumours about his mam and her fancy man. They're saying she goes into town on the bus, drinking in the Crown with some slick fella – the type of bloke her husband would call a lounge lizard if he wasn't too busy on the trawlers to think about it.

He finally drifts off, only to wake with a start when he hears a key in the door beneath his window. He looks at the glowing red digits of his alarm clock and sees it's well after two. Where the bloody hell has his da been until now? He hears his mam open the parlour door, realises she's been waiting up. She was supposed to be away over at her sister's tonight, but she must have changed her mind and come back. He can hear urgent muttering just inside the porch, heavy footsteps going down the passageway to the kitchen, then the sliding door closing with a rattle.

Art creeps along the landing. He can hear his father's voice, strangely clear and sober, his mam's voice choked up with anger and tears. He can't make out the words, but then the kitchen door slides back again and his father marches down the hall and out of the front door. His mam stands in the porch and shouts after him.

'You haven't been in't Dolphin until this time, Shaun Mainprize – in fact you haven't been in there at all.'

'I—'

'No, save yer breath, I went down to check. And you still haven't told me why you're wearing your best clobber on a Tuesday night?'

Art slips back into his room, looks out of the window, watches his da standing in the street, hands on hips. He's wearing a patterned shirt with a long, pointed collar, some kind of cream blazer, and on his feet are a pair of white slip-ons, the gold chains glinting in the moonlight.

The following day is golden bright, the sky clear, and just before midday Art meets up with Billy by the coble landing. Billy's da has asked him to take the boat out and check the lobster pots, and they've both brought sandwiches as well as their fishing gear.

Art jumps off the sea wall and looks Billy up and down. 'I see you're still wearing that bloody jacket, yer lounge lizard.'

'Will you ever shut up about it?' He shrugs off the Harrington and folds it up. 'Too hot for it anyway.'

Art follows his lead, takes off his denim jacket, and Billy reaches out to pull at the V-neck of his jumper. 'Lounge lizard yer bloody self, you look like a frigging Bay City Roller in that thing.'

'You're the lounge lizard, kidder.'

'No, YOU are. You're the frigging king of lounge lizards!'

They give each other a friendly shove and Billy stumbles

over a coil of rope. Art laughs and Billy laughs with him. He feels warm inside, blessed to have such a good mate, a friend he knows he can trust. Though he'll kill himself before he ever tells him.

After checking and rebaiting the empty pots, they set up two rods and lie back in the boat, heads resting on their folded jackets, eyes closed against the sun. They let the boat drift, neither of them talking, and Art dozes off for a while until he hears Billy's voice.

'What were yer going to tell me yesterday?'

'Eh?'

'That thing you said you were hoping to spare me from?'

'Oh, that. Nothing, kidder, I told you, I was just trying to wind you up. What did you do last night when you got in? I listened to the new Deep Purple cassette again – it's a blinder.'

'I didn't do anything really, just watched the telly. Everyone was out. My da was working on Colin Bain's boat last night – extra shift because Mousey's ill.'

Art nods. 'What about yer mam, where was she last night?'

'She were working as well, until about two in the morning I think – an extra half shift for all the shop floor. The pre-Christmas rush has started already she reckons, all the women want their new parlour curtains for the big day. She's been doing a lot of extra lately.'

Billy pauses for a moment, remembers something Seth told him that morning outside the newsagents. 'Where did your da head out to last night? Seth said he was seen getting out of a town taxi at two in the morning – in his lounge lizard gear.'

Art doesn't answer, and the silence hangs heavy, something shifting and falling into place inside their heads. Something they both hope isn't true, but which they know may become so if they utter the possibility of it out loud. It's unfamiliar territory and neither of them understands how to navigate it. The boat drifts on the calm water, a lone gull circles overhead, and the only sound is the gentle slosh against the side of the hull.

Eventually they both unpack their sandwiches and eat them without saying a word. When they've finished, Art passes Billy a Camel. Billy pulls out his lighter, catches Art's eye for a moment as he leans towards the flame, but still can't bring himself to speak. Afterwards they lie back down and both feign sleep beneath the afternoon sun. Out of the corner of his eye Art is sure he sees Billy scratch his nose, but he remains quiet and maintains the charade, doesn't ask the questions that are tumbling around in his mind.

When Billy sits up he realises they have drifted too far out, that they have almost reached the next headland. From this new vantage point everything looks different – the cottages are hidden by the pier and the long beach is a mere sliver of silver. It's an unfamiliar place, seen for the very first time, a town unravelled and sea-changed. It is a place which felt safe and solid when they left it behind that morning, yet now it appears unsure of itself, slightly unreal, as though a strong gust of wind could carry it away.

Aquarium

I meet you in the foyer of the aquarium, and for two short hours we dive deep beneath the sea. We swim through coral gardens, you and I, the mermaid-child and the merman, dancing with jellyfish in their puffball skirts, dodging the spines of purple urchins. And right at the end, just before the gift shop, we watch two stingrays fly underwater like graceful birds.

Back in the bright white light of the foyer we blink like moles and you squeeze my hand as we walk towards the exit. I want to tell you about Uncle Martin, but Mam is already waiting outside.

'Da?' I say quickly. But my voice is drowned out by the sound of waves booming through a speaker, and all the other words jump around in my mouth like slippery fish.

The late afternoon is dark as gunmetal and the sea churns and roils against the harbour wall. It would be so easy to clamber up to the top, to dive straight into the waves and never look back. I glance up at you then, see the soft line of your mouth harden as you nod at Mam. Her hand is ice against my back as she marches me away from you.

You stay by the aquarium door, stamping your feet in the packed snow, becoming smaller and smaller as we walk up the road. I turn to wave before you disappear, and you lift your hand just as Mam yanks my arm.

I remember arriving home from school each day, seeing your salt-licked boots, your frayed cap tossed over the peg. I'd throw down my satchel, punch the stiff latch and crash through the scullery, knowing you'd be hauling coal from the cellar, cheeks smudged with black dust, strangely clumsy out of water. Mam always hoped you would turn your back on the tiller, be coaxed ashore to the herring sheds, be anchored down by kipper and creel. But you wouldn't trade your fins for feet.

Now Mam drags me up the hill to the bus stop and we travel back in silence.

At home, far from the shore, I am earthbound, yet Uncle Martin always calls me his water baby. He laughs when he says it, the sound crashing over my head like something breaking. Tonight, he asks me about the aquarium, squeezes my hand, his breath warm on my face. I answer quickly, wait for him to finish speaking. When he leaves the room, I close my eyes, hold whelk shells to my ears, drown out his voice and hands with the roar of distant waves. You once told me that each shell tells a different story, but although I listen closely, they all sound the same.

Waiting to Fall

Room 409 is a dark corner room on the fourth floor, with sea views to the east and north. Ragwood Hall's website calls it a compact double, but Gina sees straight away that there's scarcely room for one person to move around, let alone two.

The gloom is partly due to the weather, and is compounded by the fact that housekeeping have left the heavy red drapes pulled halfway across the sash windows. It was raining before Gina arrived, and is even heavier now, streams of water racing down the salt-stained glass. The famed view towards the fishing village of Murrick has been obscured by low cloud, and there's little to see other than the thrashing waves at the foot of the cliffs below.

Gina has always found a certain beauty in the misery of bad weather, something dangerously seductive. She pictures herself walking along the old railway track, buffeted by the biting wind, struggling to remain upright, knowing there could be a real chance of stumbling down the steep cliffside. She opens one of the stiff sashes and looks out to sea, strains to discern the steel-grey offing beyond the curtain of rain. She is sure she can see a boat out there, a prick of light in the distance. She imagines it dashed on rocks, splintering into a handful of jackstraws, a distress flare disappearing unseen into the racing clouds.

Gina often wonders if other people visualise disasters in this way, but something has always prevented her from finding out. Deep down she knows what stops her – the fear of seeing shocked faces, of discovering she's the only one whose mind conjures up such grim scenarios. People would probably assume she spends her time wishing harm on others, yet Gina doesn't indulge in schadenfreude. She never revels in the existing misfortunes of others, she's merely unable to stop imagining the possible causes of future tragedies.

Every single day, accidents and disasters unfold before her eyes: Formula One drivers crash on her television screen, their cars exploding on impact; helicopters tumble from the skies, hurtling down towards mock-Tudor suburbia, their rotor blades tangling in telegraph wires; pedestrians step out in front of speeding cars. When miners are trapped, when buildings collapse, she pictures the bodies, crushed and lifeless, gasps when she turns on the news and sees the body count grow.

She wonders if there is some kind of subliminal logic to these unbidden thoughts – perhaps the more often she pictures death and destruction befalling others, the less chance of harm befalling her? But if so, that thinking has failed her now; her world has been knocked slightly off its axis. The only thing she can do to restore the equilibrium is make David's world rock a little too.

Gina shivers and shuts the swollen sash again, thinks how easy it would be to open it wider, to step across the low window ledge and fly down to the jagged rocks. She turns away, presses her hands against the grumbling radiator and wonders why David would pick such a desolate place to stay.

She opens her suitcase, hangs her dress on the rack next to the bathroom door. There is a small landscape on the same wall in an ornate frame, layers of oil paint yellowed with dirt and nicotine. She peers closely. A road or pathway winds into the distance across rough moorland, there is a steep cliff to the right, a glimpse of rocks and rough sea. No people or animals, no buildings or boats, no sea birds – no life at all.

The room is oppressive and Gina knows she'll go stir crazy if she stays there all afternoon. She considers going down to the lobby and ordering a coffee. She could sit in one of the leather tub chairs with her newspaper and wait for David to arrive, for her first glimpse of Sandra. But it would be risky – if he sees her it will all be over too soon.

Instead, she pulls on her walking boots, zips up her waterproof coat, finds the back stairs and walks down to the ground floor and out through the side door. From the hotel lawns she can see her bedroom windows jutting out beneath the eaves at the corner of the building. The two windows are at right angles to each other, facing east towards the sea and north towards Murrick. They form an odd wooden structure which protrudes from the stone walls, and from down below it looks flimsy, unsupported, as though it could break loose and fall over the cliff edge at any moment.

Gina walks down through the gardens to where a gate opens onto the old railway line – the "cinder track" as they call it on Ragwood's website – stretching the twenty miles between Brantbury to the south and the small seaside town of Cressburn to the north. Water is running off the banks onto the wide path, but it is still passable, quite firm underfoot, and she welcomes the whip of the wind, the beat of the rain on her face, even the cold weight of her wet jeans.

There isn't a soul in sight, and contrary to her earlier vision of a fishing boat battling the waves, the sea is an empty expanse of churned grey. There is a constant boom and roar in her ears, a feeling of pure exhilaration, the connection with something primal. She walks north for a mile or so, stumbling on the rocky path in places, the wind propelling her forward.

When she turns towards Ragwood again, her knotted hair wraps around her face and the same wind pummels her back at every step. She reaches up with both arms, hands splayed, then closes her fists as if trying to grasp the sky.

The diamond ring on her left hand glints in the fast-fading light, and she twists it between the index finger and thumb of her right hand, as though to reassure herself it is safely anchored. A small diamond, rose cut, perhaps a quarter of a carat, set in art deco platinum shoulders. For a moment she is tempted to tug it free, to throw it into the tangled thicket of bracken and bramble. But she doesn't. Instead, she allows herself to relive that night in the Spanish place; the night when David proposed. It was in Lincoln – he was there for an exhibition and had asked her to go with him – and they were tucked away in a back corner of the restaurant. They'd eaten a perfect paella cooked by Dom Pepe's wife and shared a bottle of chilled white Rioja. It was over their brandy and coffee when he pulled out the battered leather jewellery box from his jacket pocket. He placed it on the table in front of her, and as she opened it – expecting more earrings, another gold chain – he asked her to marry him.

'But—'

'It's antique, as you can see. I can't afford the modern diamond solitaire I know you'd probably prefer, but I hope you'll agree this ring is beautiful too – and very you. Gina, you're essential to my life, and I'll do anything to keep you in it. Please say yes.'

'I… Yes! But—'

He shook his head, placed his hand over hers, headed off her obvious questions.

Back in her room, Gina runs a deep bath, pours in the small bottle of hotel shower gel, arranges her wet jeans over the tepid radiator. Then she climbs into the tub, luxuriates in the hot water until it is time to get ready for dinner.

Before she dries her hair she calls reception, asks them to confirm that David Morton has arrived, says she needs to double-check he has reserved a table in the Sandpiper Restaurant for 8.30. David always books dinner for 8.30, but she wants to be sure. The receptionist doesn't question her, replies in the affirmative after checking the computer.

Her new dress is floor length, a slither of emerald silk cut on the bias, and the heels she has chosen to go with it are high. She paints her fingernails a soft oyster pink. Around her neck she wears the rose gold chain David bought her shortly after they met, and around her wrist she wears the matching bracelet he gave her for her birthday a few weeks later. Her earrings are two waterfalls of slender gold chains – a first anniversary gift.

At 7.55 she enters the restaurant, asks the maître d' if she can be seated at a table by the window. When the waiter hands her the menu she gives him her widest smile. He blushes and looks flustered, rearranges the glassware for a moment before he speaks.

'Good evening, Miss Foxton. My name is Bryan and I'll be your waiter tonight. Can I ask if this a special occasion?'

A nice touch, she thinks, calling the guests by their names. 'Please, call me Gina. And yes, it is a special occasion, Bryan – it's my birthday. However, my partner has to work tonight, so I'm all alone.'

Gina had been prepared for disappointment on her birthday, as she knew it was David's wedding anniversary the following day. Her last birthday occurred not long after they met, and he assured her then that he and his wife never did anything special to celebrate their anniversary – their celibate marriage, as he repeatedly told her, was only continuing for the sake of the children. But apparently it was still difficult for him to get away around then, as it was also his daughter's birthday, and his mother-in-law's. There were several excuses, all of the variety that would make her appear uncharitable or jealous if she challenged him.

The previous year he had still made time for her on the actual day, calling round at her apartment for a couple of hours in the evening, armed with the gold bracelet and an extravagant bouquet. But this year, despite it falling on a Friday, he told her he would be away on unavoidable business for two days in Scotland – an important client. When Gina asked if she could go with him he immediately said no; Bob from Research was going and they would travel in the same car.

David knew she had already booked her birthday as annual leave, and that she hardly knew Bob, so Gina presumed he thought it unlikely she would accost him in the corridor to check out the story. However, she had called the office that morning to speak to David's PA. She said she needed to contact him urgently about a client, that it would only take a five minute chat to sort it out, but his mobile appeared to be switched off. She added that he'd mentioned going away for his anniversary, but she'd forgotten where. Lydia told her the name of the hotel straight away, then looked up the phone number without hesitation. Gina's hunch had been correct. She immediately called the hotel and booked the cheapest room.

When David and Sandra walk into the restaurant, Gina doesn't look at them; she hides her face with her hand until they are both seated. David doesn't even glance her way, and she waits until they have ordered before she asks Bryan if she can move to the table just behind them. She tells him it's a little cold near the window and there's a draught blowing around her ankles.

From her new position she can see Sandra clearly, but David has his back to her and – unless he turns right round – is unlikely to spot her. They are sitting directly below an elaborate chandelier, dusty and unloved, several of the candle bulbs no longer working, a few of them randomly replaced with others of various sizes and shapes. Gina imagines the groan and creak, the crumbling plaster, if the glass monster were to pull free of its ceiling fixture and crash around them, splintering into a million shards. She envisages the blood running down Sandra's cheeks and neck and shoulders.

Sandra is attractive, a few years younger than Gina thought she'd be, and nothing like the image she has carried around in her head. Not that the picture in her head was bad, just different. Sandra has an air of confidence, a woman certain of her secure place in the world. She smiles often, gives David her full attention, looks at him with affection. There is nothing world-weary in that look, and there are no pained or indifferent silences at their table, only animated chatter. They are totally at ease with each other. At one point, Sandra throws her head back and laughs, then leans forward and places her hand over David's. Gina doesn't need to see David's face, Sandra's tells her all she needs to know, and although her heart is racing, she feels strangely composed – sad, yet not angry. She is suddenly unsure why she is here or what she hopes to achieve.

Bryan brings Gina's coffee to the table, and with an awkward flourish he produces a chocolate mousse. It is topped with a single candle.

'On the house,' he says. 'Happy birthday!'

Sandra watches Gina blush as she blows out the flame, then says something to David. When he turns round to look at her, his face fills with shock and confusion, then fear. It's everything she'd expected and more, but Sandra appears not to notice.

'All alone on your birthday?' she asks.

Gina nods and dabs her face with a napkin to hide her blushes. 'My… er… my partner couldn't make it tonight – work.'

'You must join us for a night cap in the bar. Mustn't she, David? A girl can't celebrate alone.'

'Oh I'm sure this young lady doesn't want to be stuck with us, Sandra,' he tries.

'Nonsense, don't be ridiculous, darling. What do you say, er…?'

'Gina.'

'Gina,' she repeats slowly. 'Pretty name. There's a girl in your office called Gina isn't there, David?'

He clears his throat and nods. 'I think she's still with us,' he says. 'I lose track to be honest.'

'Well, Gina, as you'll have gathered, I'm Sandra and this is David – and it's our anniversary tomorrow. We've been married nearly thirty years now, so we're quite the old hands. But do you know, I actually believe staying with one person offers far more variety than a string of different relationships can.'

David looks embarrassed. 'I'm sure this young lady doesn't want to listen to your counselling speeches, darling.'

Sandra laughs. 'Yes, sorry Gina, I was starting to talk shop there – I'm a Relate counsellor for my sins! Anyway, needless to say we'd be delighted to combine our celebration with yours in some way. So please do say yes to a drink in the bar.'

'I'd love to, Sandra – thank you.'

The Puffin Bar is in the basement, strangely out of kilter with the rest of the hotel. The ceilings are low, the walls exposed stone, and there is nothing at all to suggest how the bar got its name. They sit on low stools at a brass-topped table, the room empty except for a couple who look as though they'd rather be somewhere else.

David orders three brandies, perches uncomfortably on the edge of his seat and looks everywhere but at Gina. Sandra talks about their anniversary, how they are meeting friends and family in an exclusive restaurant for lunch the following day. She tells Gina they have been married for twenty-eight years, that she has never regretted marrying him, not even for an hour. Gina wonders if that's true, yet knows it doesn't really matter – the fact she has said it is enough.

She asks Gina about her own relationships. Gina finds herself telling Sandra about Paul and Ian, Ted and Karl, embellishing her stories with wild exaggeration and amusing anecdotes as she describes each successive breakup, revelling all the while in David's obvious discomfort.

When she reaches the end of her final story, Sandra leans forward, rests her warm fingertips on Gina's wrist.

'There are all sorts of clever sayings and theories about relationships, Gina, but do you want to know what life has taught me – and my years as a counsellor?'

Gina nods, though she's pretty certain she doesn't want to know.

'Well, it's common sense if you think about it. When you're first with someone you tell them all your finest stories, you dazzle and surprise them with your wit and originality, show them every one of your best moves. It's a big trick you pull off, a system you develop to fall head over heels in love – with yourself as much as anyone else – and you do it over and over again. So I—'

'Sandra,' David interrupts, 'stop forcing your theories down this poor girl's throat. Do you want another drink?'

Sandra flaps him away with her hand and carries on talking.

'So I know it's easy to make someone think you are essential to their lives – that you are more fascinating, more beautiful, than anyone they have ever met. But once you've got them there, you're just waiting to fall. Because sooner or later, that guy, that woman, is going to see you acting like a fool, and that's when they'll make the choice to move on or stick with you.'

She pauses for a moment, presses her fingers harder into Gina's wrist.

'It's hard to get past that, Gina, because that's when the old stories and the old moves no longer work. Not many of us make it through that tricky time, but those of us who do… well, we understand we have something pretty special, something worth hanging on to for dear life.'

Back in her room, Gina snaps on the main light and makes a drink. She needs a coffee to sober up. She catches sight of the painting again, wonders why such a dull and dated picture would survive successive room makeovers. Then she realises it is actually the view from her window towards Murrick, but the odd perspective means Murrick is not even in the painting.

She takes it down from the wall and lays it on the bed, studying it for a while. Then she removes a leaflet for Cressburn's botanical gardens from the guest folder, and with her nail scissors she cuts out the tiny figure of a woman from one of the photographs. She picks up her bottle of nail polish from the bedside table and dabs a small pink circle on the back of the woman's head, then sticks her upside down on the rocks at the foot of the cliffs, folding and twisting her legs and arms.

She rehangs the painting and goes over to the window, sees the rain pooled on the low ledge where it has driven underneath the badly fitting sash. Then she yanks the carpet free from its tacks, pulls it away from the corner, lies down and puts her ear to the dusty floorboards. She feels the draught on her cheek, hears the moan of the sea, knows there is nothing between her and the cliffs save for these creaking boards and a thin layer of lath and plaster. Gina pictures the flash and crack of lightning, the entire wooden structure heaving itself free from the wall, carrying her with it to the rocks below. She curls up in the corner and waits to fall.

Shining Brighter

He leaves you in the heat of summer, yet you know he isn't sure, is still testing out his new life with a foot firmly wedged in the old life's door. You watch him carry boxes to the car, see him glance up at the window as he drives away, as he heads towards the flat in Camden Town.

You light your first cigarette in the silent room, already pining – not for him, but for the coast and moors, for your familiar northern stars.

You call the office to book an extra day's leave, set off for King's Cross to catch the 12.22. You are shocked to feel relief and grief in equal measure, to observe that both emotions are as true, surprised to see the city in a kinder light, to notice the sun shining brighter.

You buy a cheese roll, a coffee – sweetened for the shock – then find your seat in coach B just before the train pulls away, somehow half-expecting to see him there on the platform, waving, smiling, until you are out of sight.

In your hometown, down at the water's edge, lulled by the cadence of the waves, you are relieved to find the parting has emptied you of him. And in the pub you talk of this and that, of something and nothing, your lips stained Rioja red, yet you don't mention he's left, don't speak of him at all.

Back in Archway there are flowers and a card from work.

Cheer up! it reads – no one having quite known what to say – and you realise you'll be okay, now that you can finally be yourself again.

You try to picture him in Camden Town with the girl from Madrid, the girl who fiercely coveted him, whose name you couldn't bear to say aloud. But however hard you focus, their faces drift like windblown sand.

When you hear his car pull up to the door, you slide both bolts across and sit quietly on the stairs until he's gone.

Straight in the Eye

Beth and James arrived in the Japanese Alps after yet another petty argument. It had started before they left Tokyo and then worsened when they reached Shinshimashima train station and were unable to agree on the bus route up to Kamikochi. When they finally found the right bus, a previous disagreement resurfaced regarding their accommodation. Beth had wanted to stay in a hotel, but James had insisted on the log cabins at the edge of the campsite. He won in the end, but when she was tired and hungry she started grizzling about his choice again.

Beth read in their guide book that there was a healthy population of bears in Kamikochi, but no one they spoke to at the campsite had seen one. That evening they sat outside in the half-light of dusk and listened to the macaques chattering in the trees. Yet Beth couldn't settle, sure there were bears all around them, convinced they would come down to the cabins in search of food in the night, that they would rummage through the remains of barbeques and tear the lids off bins. When they went to bed, their hair scented with woodsmoke from the camp fire, she lay awake until the early hours, listening out for the slightest noise, watching the moon through the skylight.

She thought about getting up, considered taking James's mobile from the shelf at the side of his futon so she could check his messages and calls. But Beth knew she had to start trusting him again, that she couldn't spend her whole life suspecting him, searching his pockets, monitoring his phone, inventing scenarios in her head. He told her he had ended things with Tanya, that he wanted them to try again, that now it was up to her. So she had a choice. She could believe him, or make plans to leave him, or spend every waking hour worrying about where he was and what he was doing. Or she could do all of those things in turn, as she had been doing for the past two months. It was easy for James to say that it was "up to her". It was and it wasn't. Her heart was broken, yet she still loved him. He seemed to think she could click her fingers and forgive and forget, that they could move on and not look back. Beth knew it was too soon to forgive him, yet for the next three weeks she was determined to try and forget. She didn't want to spoil the trip they had been planning for over two years.

When they walked across to the café for breakfast they noticed signs at the visitor centre which chalked up details of recent bear sightings: *None*, and offered safety advice: *Please walk with the bell for giving bear notice!*

The campsite shop was filled with a plethora of jangling *kumayoke suzu* and Beth insisted they bought a small red bell. However, they still set off unarmed, James having decided that the constant clanking would disturb the birds they hoped to see, and scare off the elusive *kamoshika* mountain goats. He wrapped the bell in a bandana to stop it jangling, then tucked it in the side pocket of his rucksack. Beth was still unsure, but somehow everything seemed safer when the sun was shining and crowds of Japanese tourists were strolling back and forth along the paths.

Their day's climb started at Taisho Pond, a place Beth found strangely haunting. Blackened, withered trees reached up out of the clear water, a reminder that the lake was formed by the last eruption of a nearby active volcano. James had picked up a map of the different walking trails in the visitor centre, and Beth followed him up the lower slopes through the trees, jumping at the snap of a twig or the whir of a bird's wings. James climbed fast, striding ahead, and as the canopy became denser and the forest darkened, Beth became more nervous. She wanted to turn back even though she knew she was being foolish, and she found herself constantly looking over her shoulder, then up towards where the tree line ended, convinced she could see shapes moving in the gloom.

After two hours of climbing they emerged from the forest, and Beth stopped for a few moments in the sudden warmth, catching her breath before the final ascent, any fear of bears dissipated by the sunshine. James carried on, scrambling up the scree towards the higher path. He turned and shouted to her as he reached the top of the ridge.

'The first of the mountain huts is up here, Beth, exactly where I thought!' He pointed with his walking pole. 'I'll see you there.'

She scrambled up the slopes, stopping occasionally to admire alpine flowers, turning to gaze at the view below as she put some distance between herself and the tree line. She found the path between the rocks and followed the route James had just taken. As she climbed the last fifty metres she was sure she heard the brief high-pitched beep of a text notification, and the sound filled her with dread and suspicion. When she reached the plateau of flat-topped stones she caught James slipping his phone back into his pocket. He walked towards her, his whole face flushed with guilt and embarrassment, and she felt her stomach twist.

'Let's have our rice snacks and water,' he said quickly. 'There's a great place to sit in front of the hut – fabulous views.'

She followed him and sat down on the flat rocks, her heart still racing, her ribcage aching with the familiar foreboding. Still high above them were the snow-capped peaks of Hotaka, and below them the river flowed like mercury through the valley. Yet in the distance, barely perceptible wisps of white smoke hung in the still air above the sleeping fire dragon of Yakedake volcano, and Beth found herself shivering despite the warm autumn sunshine.

'Was that your phone I heard?' she asked.

'Phone? Do you really think there'd be a signal up here? You're becoming paranoid, Beth. Don't spoil the day.'

'Me? *Me* spoil the day? It's you who's made me paranoid. I'm on edge all the time, wondering about every text and every call, about where you are when you're late home from work. If you've nothing to hide then look me straight in the eye and tell me she hasn't contacted you. Better still, let me see your phone messages.'

'Don't be ridiculous, Beth.' He laughed, but he didn't make eye contact with her, he looked up at the mountains instead.

She held out her hand. 'Go on, give the phone to me. Show me you're innocent.'

'You're being…' He suddenly faltered, lifted his hand in greeting to someone on the slope above – a man in a red jacket waving a silver walking pole.

James stood up. 'Quit it now, Beth, this guy is heading over here.'

'I know it's still going on, James, I absolutely know,' she hissed.

As she finished speaking, the climber arrived at the hut, announcing his presence with the clanking of a large bear bell. Beth managed to feign a smile as he introduced himself, but she left most of the talking to James. Motoki spoke little

English, but when he ran out of vocabulary the three of them communicated with exaggerated gestures. They both laughed too loudly and nodded too wildly, and when Beth did join in the conversation there was a brittle brightness to her words.

They offered their new acquaintance chocolate, and he offered a flask of green tea in return. Beth and James didn't exchange a word between them as they packed away the remains of their food, and when they set off they began their slow descent close on Motoki's heels. As they walked in silence, Beth completely forgot about the possibility of bears, her mind still whirring, wondering if James was telling the truth and if she was simply being paranoid. After all, was it likely there was a phone signal on the top of a mountain?

Deep in thought, she was caught off guard when Motoki's outstretched arm brought them to an abrupt standstill. They froze midstep as though competing in a game of musical statues. When she looked up, her eye was caught by a dense black rock just above the tree line. It stood out against the pale scree, and when she refocused, the boulder became bear. She could make out the tilt and sway of his salt and pepper muzzle as he tried to catch their scent, and the glint of eyes like polished coals. When they stumbled to a halt there was a mesmeric moment as he continued to walk towards them. As he reared up onto his hind legs, Beth swore he looked her straight in the eye, poised and sure, calmly weighing up his options. Not afraid to let her see what he was thinking, quite prepared to show his cards, to be clear about his intentions.

Then Motoki jangled the bell on his rucksack, and just as swiftly as he'd turned towards them, the bear dropped to the ground and loped away without looking back.

Dizzy with adrenaline, they remained motionless, stiff as statues, until Motoki gestured down the mountainside with sweeping arm movements to indicate that they should keep moving. Beth scrambled after him, pleased to have company and not to be alone with James, happy with their enforced silence, relieved to listen to nothing except the clamorous clanking of the bear bell until they reached the campsite.

James dropped a short way behind them to take some final photographs of the views across the mountains in the afternoon light. It was the last chance to see Yakedake before they were plunged deep into the forest again. Beth turned back at one point, reluctant to lose sight of him despite her current anger, but James waved her on, told her he'd catch up with them, shook his belt to show her he'd clipped on the bear bell they had bought that morning.

At the edge of the trees, Beth stopped for a moment, sure she had heard something behind her: rocks tumbling; scree scattering; a muffled cry, eerily human; a soft growl. The sounds echoed across the mountain in the stillness, and her heart raced. She tried to call out, but the words stuck in her throat, and when she listened again all she could hear was the fading tinkle of a bell.

She knew she should go back up the path to check on James, that she should shout ahead and ask Motoki to wait. But she couldn't do either. Instead, she kept up a steady pace towards the trees, watching the bright red jacket which bobbed ahead of her, leading her down into the cover of the forest.

The Right Castanets

In the summer of 1968, when Alice turned fourteen, her parents rented a villa on the outskirts of a fishing village in Catalonia. Her mother had been learning Spanish at night classes, but their maid, Maria, always tilted her head to one side when she spoke to her, frowning a little, as though she didn't understand. But Alice knew she was pretending, that she knew perfectly well what her mother was saying.

The villa was white with dark green shutters. There was a large table in the kitchen where they sat down each evening to eat olives and fresh anchovies while they watched Maria prepare their meal. Alice's mother gave her money for the shopping every morning, and she would bring back loaves of dense bread with thick dark crusts, cloth bags of rice, and iridescent fish straight from the quayside.

Maria was raven-haired with glowing skin, and Alice was strangely unsettled by her overt sexuality. When she caught Maria looking at her she felt somehow inadequate, and she always left the room quickly if they found themselves alone together.

One evening Alice's parents told Maria to take the night off and they drove inland up into the mountains. Her father had heard there was a fiesta in the next town. They stopped en route at a village bodega, its inside musty and cool after the heat of the day. Alice and her mother sat at tables fashioned from wine casks, and her father stayed at the bar, chatting in broken English to the barman. He was slim-hipped and liquid-eyed, and there was something about him in his tight black trousers and fitted white shirt which made Alice blush when he smiled. When her mother sent her across to ask for more drinks, her father told Alice that Juan would bring them over to their table.

'The barman is called Juan,' she said as she sat back down.

Her mother pursed her lips. 'They are all called Juan,' she said drily, 'and you are too young to be thinking about the names of waiters.'

When they arrived in the fiesta town the streets were filled with the smell of garlic, fish and spicy sausage. The men were cooking large pans of paella in the main square. Women wore tiered dresses splashed with bold polka dots; gold hoop earrings; turquoise flowers in their oiled hair. They had crimson lips and flashing eyes, flicked fans with slender wrists. They seemed alien to Alice; knowing and bold. Like Maria.

There was music playing in the streets, laughter coming from the doorways of the bars and cafés. Alice wanted to buy castanets from a street vendor. They were roughly carved, decorated with pictures of toreadors and flamenco dancers, stained with a thick varnish, threaded together with coarse, coloured string. But her father said they were selling at an inflated price for the fiesta, that he would buy her some in the village the following day.

On the drive back she thought about Juan, imagined walking with him in the moonlight along the beach, his hand in hers, the tan of his skin against the paleness of her own. She remembered the boy she kissed after the school dance the week before they came away: the heat of him through the thin cotton of his shirt as he pressed against her, the hardness of him, the give of him, the firm pressure of his lips against hers. And the feeling inside her, a sweet softness she wanted to hold onto, the promise of something elusive, something still out of her reach.

As good as his word her father bought her some castanets the following morning when he went out for his newspaper.

But when Alice held them in her hand she was disappointed. They were the wrong castanets. These were plastic, and the pictures were not hand-painted, they were transfers. But she knew her father didn't know the difference, or think that it mattered. So she tried to look grateful and said nothing.

In the afternoon, she took them down to the beach to practise, imagined she was Maria, that she was dancing with Juan, her body twisting in time to some imaginary flamenco beat. She clacked the castanets in time to the rhythm in her head until her mother lost her temper. But no matter how hard she tried she couldn't get them to sound like the ones she had heard at the fiesta.

Eventually she went back across to the villa to find her father, hoping to persuade him to forego his siesta and sit with her in the gardens. It was the time of day she liked being in the villa best, when Maria had gone home between her shifts, when Alice could relax, take a cold drink from the fridge without the woman's eyes appraising her.

The house was silent, and she walked through the kitchen to the hallway. Then she heard a stifled cry and low voices. The sound was coming from her parents' room, and she walked the length of the corridor and carefully opened the door.

Juan and her father were both on the bed. Her father was lying down, his head thrown back, and Juan was knelt over him, his back to Alice. For a moment, unsure what she was watching, Alice froze in the doorway. Then she swung round, confused and embarrassed, kicking the doorframe in her rush.

Both men turned at the sound, her father hastily pulling the crumpled sheet up to his waist. He muttered something and Juan jumped to his feet.

'Er… darling, wait,' her father stuttered.

Alice swung back round for a second, hoping for an explanation which would somehow make sense of this, yet already knowing there wasn't one which could.

'Juan was just passing, and I… I asked him in for a drink. But then I knocked it over – over him I mean – and so… and so I'm lending him some clothes. No harm done – we don't need to tell your mother do we, sweetheart?'

Alice turned away again, stumbled out into the corridor, slamming the door. As she raced to the kitchen, her father caught up with her and grabbed her arm, his other hand still clutching the sheet.

'We'll go to the shops tomorrow and I'll buy you something nice – that sun hat you saw the other day? What do you say, Alice?'

She pulled away from him and ran out of the villa without answering, her eyes blurring with tears. She knew her mother would sense something was wrong straight away, so she walked down to the shoreline and paced back and forth across the bay.

The next morning they went into town together. She usually enjoyed spending time on her own with her father, but today Alice would have preferred to have been on the beach with her mother. She had tried not to think about what she had seen in the villa the previous afternoon; part of her had succeeded in blanking it out, part of her had convinced herself it was nothing, that it was as he'd said. But a bigger part of her knew this wasn't true.

As they walked along the main street he tried to catch hold of her hand, but it felt clammy and she pulled away, pretending to look in a shop window.

At the front of the colourful display were the perfect castanets, the ones she had wanted all along. They were carved from wood, decorated by hand, tied together with plaited yellow and red string.

Yet as her father paid for them, along with the sun hat she had chosen, Alice felt no delight in her new gifts, no thrill at finally owning the right castanets. When he handed her the bag his nervous smile reminded her of the times he arrived home late from somewhere with a hastily bought bunch of roses for her mother. She always tutted and threw them to one side, muttering about empty gestures and broken promises.

Back out on the street he took a photograph of Alice in her new hat, clutching the castanets in their bright paper package. She scowled at him, and when he cajoled her to smile, told her how pretty she looked, she replied that the sun was in her eyes.

When she opened the parcel back at the villa, the castanets looked tacky. There were splinters of wood where they had not been sanded down properly, the varnish was badly applied and had dried in drips, and the picture of the bull-fighter was just another reminder of Juan and his flashing eyes. She knew they were identical to the ones she'd coveted at the fiesta, yet everything else was no longer the same.

She left them on the kitchen table, and when Maria returned in the afternoon to cook their evening meal she sneered as she picked them up. Alice snatched them from her hand, hid them at the bottom of a drawer beneath her T-shirts, and when they returned home she left them behind along with her new sun hat.

A week later, when their holiday photographs were collected from the chemist, her father held out the one of her standing outside the shop. 'I haven't seen your hat or those castanets since we came back, sweetheart?'

She took the photograph from him and pretended to study it closely, suddenly remembering what her mother always used to say when he arrived home with the petrol station roses.

'No, I decided to leave them behind, Daddy. I can't be bought that cheaply,' she said.

A Small Thing to Carry

They say that every journey starts with some kind of promise, and when I first arrived in Bratislava I headed up to the Slavin Memorial to keep the one I'd made to Kristina, my late grandmother's cousin.

The sun was strong, and a soft haze shimmered above the streets that snaked up the city's highest hill. I'd first glimpsed the obelisk from the old town below. It was partly obscured by trees and too distant to make out clearly, but I knew from my guidebook that it was topped by a Russian soldier trampling the Nazi flag underfoot.

When Kristina heard I'd be visiting Slovakia on my summer trip, she asked if I would find her brother's grave in the military cemetery beneath the memorial. She gave me a copy of a photograph to keep, taken on their farm before the war: the two of them smiling, hands in their pockets, a cigarette dangling from the corner of Vasily's mouth, and a second photograph of him in his uniform, which she wanted me to leave at the foot of the headstone.

'I wouldn't ask,' she said, 'but it's only a small thing to carry.'

When I reached the top of the hill I walked slowly along each identical row of rough-hewn gravestones, searching for the name. Although my grandmother once taught me a little Russian, Kristina knew I was slow to decipher Cyrillic, and before I left she gave me a card with her brother's name neatly printed on it.

And then I saw it: *Vasily Ivankov.*

The grave was neatly kept yet bare, and I noticed there were candles atop many of the others close by. There was also a framed photograph of a young soldier propped up against the neighbouring headstone. I crouched down to take a closer look, worked out that his Christian name was Pavel. He was lathe-thin and achingly handsome, and although he was standing proud, posing for the camera in his freshly pressed uniform, there was no swagger or arrogance about him. His guileless face was full of hope. Despite the fact I knew it was unlikely, I couldn't help hoping that he and Vasily had shared tobacco and stories, all their dreams of home, as they fought side by side to free the city.

I moved back across to Vasily's grave, took out Kristina's newly framed photograph of him and placed it in front of the stone. As I stood up, I heard footsteps approaching, and a man stopped at Pavel's grave. He was around my own age – the age Vasily and most of the other young soldiers would have been when they lost their lives in 1945 – and carrying a beautiful handmade hiking staff. He nodded, knelt down by the grave and placed a bunch of wildflowers on the grass, then bowed his head for a moment as though in prayer. The cemetery was almost deserted, and when he looked up we nodded again, smiled in recognition of the coincidence. He introduced himself as Timur, repeating '*dedushka*' – grandfather – as he pointed at the headstone. I suggested to him that the two soldiers may have been friends, but his accent was so thick that I was unsure of his answer.

Timur saw I was struggling to understand, held up his hand for me to wait as he searched his rucksack. He produced a card, typed in English on one side and German on the other. The translation was a little rough, but the basic story was clear. Timur was selling Soviet memorabilia to help fund his journey around Eastern Europe. His father was gravely ill, and anxious to entrust his son with all the important family stories before they were forgotten, wanting him to visit the places which had played a part in the family's history. His father perhaps hoped he would be able to see them one last time, through his son's eyes, before he passed away. As I read the card, Timur nodded encouragement, spreading out a motley collection of bric-a-brac on the grass in front of his grandfather's headstone. There was nothing I wanted, but it was hard to refuse a man who had shared his story; a man whose family may well be linked with my own.

When I hesitated, he reached in his pocket for something else, and pressed a metal cross into my palm, fashioned from patterned tin. '*Dedushka*,' he said again, pointing at the grave. 'You have.'

For a moment I was overwhelmed, and then I responded in the only way I could, by handing him my copy of Kristina's photograph of her and Vasily. 'For you,' I said.

He looked momentarily puzzled, unsure what to do or how to react. Then he smiled, nodded and thanked me, slipped the photograph into his pocket as he retrieved his trinkets from the grass, suddenly anxious to leave. He hoisted his rucksack over one shoulder and gave me a quick wave as he strode away, disappearing from view behind the obelisk.

I wanted to go after him, felt there was something I had misunderstood, but he was a stranger, unknowable, and the language barrier was too high a fence to climb. Instead, I sat down on a nearby bench and ran my finger down the length of the cross, as though the pattern was a form of braille which would reveal the final story of Vasily and of Timur's grandfather, as though it would help me understand what these young soldiers saw and felt as they fought for the freedom of a foreign city. But all I could think about were the ghosts of lives lost too soon, lives unlived. And Timur.

Timur's typed card said his grandfather's family were originally from a village near Lake Baikal. I thought of a film I'd seen of the lake – water so clear you could see to the bottom even where it was forty metres deep, and in winter you could skate across ice as transparent as glass. I imagined Pavel as a teenager, fishing with his father, shyly courting a girl from the next village. And more than anything, I wanted to hear more about Timur's family, wished he hadn't rushed away, still wondered if I'd said something wrong. A small cloud blocked the sun for a moment. I'd never felt as lonely as I did right then.

That same evening, I sat outside a restaurant in Hviezdoslav Square and watched the crowds making the most of the warm weather. Yet my mind kept going back to Timur. I found myself searching for him among the passers-by, looking twice every time I saw a tall man, a blond man, a man carrying a rucksack. I shouldn't have let him go. His family and mine were connected somehow – I could feel it. Even if Vasily and Pavel hadn't known each other, they'd both been part of something that linked us all together, that incredible human sacrifice in the name of freedom.

When I walked back to my hotel I passed a church with a small graveyard at the front. It was almost dark, yet an elderly woman was lighting a candle at the foot of a tall memorial. By her side was Timur.

My heart lurched and I almost called out. I half-lifted my hand to wave, but something stopped me, and a part of me already understood that the scene I was about to witness would change everything. I watched Timur talk to the woman as he opened his rucksack and held out several small items. She nodded in reply to him, then selected one of the trinkets. When she held it up I could see it was a cheap tin cross. I closed my fingers around its replica in my pocket.

Had I been deceived, or had I misunderstood? Had I shaped Timur's words and gestures into the story I wanted to hear? Oddly, it didn't seem to matter now. The cross was a small thing to carry, and I knew I would treasure it anyway.

People Like You

When I take the room service order up to 409, there are only ten minutes to go before the end of my shift. Our staff accommodation is at the other end of the same corridor, so I decide it would be pointless to trek right back down to the kitchen.

I almost trip up as I come out of the service lift – there's a permanent ruck in the carpet that no amount of pulling or stretching will flatten and it catches me out nearly every time. The plate of sandwiches slides to the edge of the tray, but I manage to keep it straight as I right myself, at the same time grabbing hold of the teetering bottle of Chablis.

Mrs Holfer answers the door immediately, as though she's been waiting at the other side with her eye fixed to the peephole.

I put the tray down on the bed, as there's nowhere else to leave it in this room. I've tried to balance it on the bedside table before but there isn't enough space.

She picks up the wine, twists off the cap and pours a glass straight away, doesn't even wait for me to leave before she takes a drink.

'That's better,' she says, brightly. 'Thank you, Bryan.'

I notice the room is cold, that one of the sash windows is propped open with a book.

'Is everything okay, Mrs Holfer – would you like me to close the window? It's started to rain.'

She pulls her cardigan around her as though she has only just noticed the cold, but shakes her head.

'No thank you, I'm fine. The fresh sea air blows the cobwebs away. And I've told you before – call me Adele.'

I smile and nod, then turn to leave. 'Enjoy your sandwiches, Mrs… er, Adele. I'm going off shift now, but if you need anything else just call down to reception.'

As I walk towards the door I notice the small landscape painting on the wall by the bathroom. Someone has stuck a cut-out figure of a woman onto the rocks at the foot of the cliffs. She's upside down, and they've twisted the arms and legs in different directions so they look broken. I turn back to look at Mrs H but I already know it's not her work. Housekeeping must have missed it this morning – weekend changeovers are often a bit dodgy. I guess Minnie was in the Puffin Bar after hours last night and cleaned her rooms from inside a hangover cloud. I pull at it with my finger and thumb and it peels away quite easily. Mrs H raises an eyebrow but she doesn't say anything.

'Have a nice evening, Bryan!'

I turn as I reach the door. 'You too.'

'And if you fancy a nightcap you know where to find me.'

She reaches under the edge of the bed and brandishes a bottle of Jack Daniels.

'Oh, yeah, er… thanks. Breakfast shift for me tomorrow though, so probably need an early night.'

She smiles, unfazed. 'Young people like you – good-looking, confident, your lives stretching ahead of you – you don't realise how quickly it will all slip away. Ah well, the offer still stands if you change your mind.'

She's not so bad is Mrs H – Adele. She stays at Ragwood quite often. She says she comes here for the sea air, for some peace and quiet, to read and walk on the moors. She tells me she likes room 409 because of the view, but I think it's because it's cheap and near to the staff quarters. For all her saying she enjoys the solitude, I reckon she's been a little lonely since her divorce. Staff turnover is high here, and rumour has it that she's managed to seduce a couple of the kitchen lads in her time. She's in pretty good shape really for a woman that old. Pushing forty I reckon – nearly twice my age. Still, I can see why you wouldn't say no if it was on offer.

I walk back along the corridor and push the swing door marked *Private.* Once inside my room I pull off my jacket and bow tie, slip on a warm jumper, then lie down on the bed. I look up at the stained ceiling and listen to the rain lashing against the glass. It's forecast to turn to snow later on.

I'm not sure why I've stuck it out at Ragwood Hall in this strange, bleak landscape, but the contrast with chocolate box Oxfordshire is perhaps reason enough. I needed to get away from there – where nothing bad or interesting ever happened – and this was the first job I saw which offered accommodation. I didn't realise how isolated it would be up here, or how far north it was, or that I'd have to buy a moped to get around. And I thought I'd be doing more than just working and getting drunk, fumbling my way through the occasional one-night stand. But at least everything here feels authentic, substantial, and I'm not being suffocated day after day. I just wish I could find someone to connect with, that life would start happening for real.

After a few minutes I hear voices in the corridor – Martin and Lisa coming off their shifts. One set of footsteps stops outside my door for a few seconds and I imagine I can hear Lisa breathing at the other side of the thin panelling. But no one knocks.

I must've drifted off, because the next thing I know it's eight o'clock and there are more heavy footsteps outside before the swing door bangs.

I think about what to do. Should I go down to the bar later – staff are allowed in the back room of the Puffin – or should I make an effort and go to the Wyke Arms in the next village? The Puffin Bar is a bit crap to be honest; it has a cold, desperate feel to it and all the conversation revolves around work. Plus there's always Lisa, staring at me with those doe eyes. I only slept with her the once, when we were both drunk, but now she thinks I owe her something.

The Wyke Arms is quite special – a warren of cosy rooms, all red velvet and burnished brasses, old beams and log fires. Yeah, I know, it sounds like a cliché, but the landlord plays brilliant music from the seventies and there's a stack of great books in one of the alcoves. He's let me borrow a few: Steinbeck, Hemingway, Kafka – turns out those old guys had really important stuff to say.

There's something about the Wyke that's like coming home; it wraps you up in a warm blanket, shines like a friendly beacon when everything else around here often feels a little alien and off-kilter. I long for another kind of life when I'm in the Wyke. My grandad has a saying which kind of sums it up: "the deep peace of a quiet hearth". Or maybe it's Della behind the bar who makes me long for that different life. Della is everything Lisa isn't.

I look out of the window again – it's really dark tonight and although the rain has stopped I'm sure I can see a few flakes of snow twirling in the light at the end of the driveway. It's not a great evening to take out the moped, but at least there's no real danger of getting pulled for drink-driving out here. Sod it, I'll go.

I push Della to accept a lift at closing time, even though I know I shouldn't. I'm quite drunk for one thing, and it's snowing for God's sake. I wave my spare helmet at her, even though it's obvious she's better off going home in the barman's car. But despite everything, I'm still hoping she might come back with me – it's quite easy to sneak guests in up the staff stairs – and, well… you know.

So I mess everything up big time – she ends up calling me a bully – and Geoff, the barman, looks as though he's about to punch me. 'People like you,' he says, spluttering, 'people like you come up here to work at Ragwood and just think you can do as you please. Always drunk, sleeping around – then you bugger off back to wherever it is you come from leaving behind a trail of destruction.'

I watch them drive off, the Toyota's rear lights disappearing around the bend. Then the lights go out in the pub and the dark road suddenly feels less familiar, more treacherous. The snow is still little more than a dusting, but it's falling faster now. I skid as I set off, ease off on the throttle and try to take it slow. As I round the corner at the bottom of the first hill I feel the back wheel sliding away, and before I can try and correct it I'm laid out on the road, the wet snow soaking straight through my jeans. I'm not really hurt, just a scrape on my elbow, and I pick up the bike and set off again. I imagine Della leaning against Geoff in the car, kissing him goodnight outside her parents' farm. I grit my teeth and keep going, relieved when I see the hotel looming up ahead.

As I put my bike in the shed, I see there's a light on in 409. The windows jut out from the corner of the building, looking both east to the sea and north across the moors to Murrick. The curtains aren't drawn, and I imagine I see a shape move across the room.

I take the service lift to the top floor and push open the swing door. There's music coming from Lisa's room and I can hear low voices. I know I won't be able to get to my own room without them hearing – the floorboards squeak and my door bangs shut however careful you are – but I can't face seeing anyone right now. I turn round, look down the unlit corridor towards Adele Holfer's room. There's still a light showing underneath the door.

I shrug off my wet jacket and hang it on the fire extinguisher by the lift, comb my hair in the mirror opposite, notice a scratch on my face which must have happened when I dropped the moped. I lick my finger, wipe the thin trail of blood away, then unlace my muddy boots and leave them near my jacket, pad quietly along the corridor in my socks.

I knock softly, see the shadow of Mrs H's feet as she stands at the peephole.

She opens the door halfway. I notice her face is scrubbed clean of makeup and she's wearing a bright silk kimono. She raises her eyebrows and looks at me questioningly.

'I thought I'd take you up on that offer of a drink.'

She glances at the clock. 'It's a bit late, Bryan,' she whispers. 'And what happened to your cheek – it's scratched? And you're all wet?'

She steps aside to let me in the room, closes the door quietly.

'It's nothing,' I say. 'I just dropped my moped in the snow – no real damage done.'

There's a book open on her bed, splayed face down – Russian short stories. No sign of the bottle of Jack.

'Were you waiting up for me?' I ask, stupidly.

She shakes her head and smiles. 'No, I was reading. I shouldn't have invited you in the first place – I guess I was feeling a bit down. My books are good company, but sometimes I need a little conversation. You'd better get to bed, Bryan – you're drunk.'

I laugh at my stupidity for getting it so wrong, but she thinks I'm laughing at her.

She frowns. 'I know you probably think I'm—'

'No, no, whatever you're going to say, I'm not thinking it. I just wanted to talk. I messed up tonight. When I was out, I mean. I thought you might understand... ' I trail off, knowing I've blown it with Mrs H too, even though I'm telling the truth.

Strangely, I feel like crying. 'People like me... well, we mess things up quite a lot...'

'People like you? Don't lump yourself in with everyone else, Bryan. There are no people like you – you're unique. And witty and clever and good company when you're not drunk and feeling sorry for yourself.'

Something softens in her face then and she reaches up, strokes my cheek. 'Go to bed now. Whatever happened at the pub it will all seem better tomorrow.'

The following morning is a beauty. The hotel lawns, the distant moors, the village rooftops, have all been dusted with snow as fine as icing sugar, and the sky is the kind of straightforward blue that promises a fresh start.

When I enter the dining room, I'm surprised to see Adele is already sitting at her table. She smiles when she sees me.

'Good morning, Bryan.'

'Good morning. I'm really sorry about—'

She cuts me off, reaches for my arm as I take out my order pad. 'What time do you come off shift this morning?'

'I'll be off at eleven.'

'I was wondering if you'd like to come for a drive with

me over the moors – it's too good a day to miss. I think you said you enjoyed reading? There's a wonderful secondhand bookshop in Murrick, and a fish shack further up the coast where they only cook the catch of the day – though you'll need to wrap up warm. There are sometimes seal pups around there at this time of year.'

I don't answer her straight away, but I know I'm smiling like an idiot. I've got that feeling inside me like the one the Wyke Arms gives me – or used to give me – only better. She looks at me questioningly. 'Well?'

'Well yes… yes please. I'm not back on shift until 6.30. So yeah, I'd love to come for a drive with you, Mrs Holf—'

'I've told you before – call me Adele.'

In the Time It Takes to Make a Risotto

Isla sits down at the table, watches the blade of Sam's knife glitter beneath the spotlights. Curved and sharp, it slices through the translucent flesh of pale green shallots, the velvety skin of forest mushrooms, three creamy cloves of garlic. She wishes he'd sit down for a moment, tell her about his business trip, yet she knows he's busying himself in the kitchen so he doesn't have to talk to her, even though he must be tired, having only arrived back from Munich that same afternoon.

Isla reaches for her phone and scrolls through the local newspaper for headlines, frowns as she reads about a serious assault in Primrose Park. She flicks back and forth until her eye is caught by this week's advice column.

Dear Debbie, should I tell my husband about my affair with his best friend?

She looks up, guilt burning her cheeks as though she'd spoken aloud, but Sam has turned away from the counter to reach for the sauté pan.

It's almost a year since Ged ended their relationship. They were infatuated with each other for a while, but he couldn't bear to carry on deceiving his childhood friend. Isla has buried the details of their unpleasant break-up, blanked out the shameful memories of her desperate pleading, yet she can't let go of those summer afternoons at his apartment in town; the slip and glide of his sweat-licked skin against hers, the heat and noise from the tapas bar below. Those stolen hours still breathe inside her, they dance to their own flamenco beat, flutter their wings against her ribcage.

She glances back down at the advice column, reads the response, relieved to discover that Debbie advises against owning up. Isla can't comprehend why anyone would want to tell their partner about an affair – particularly if it was long since over. Unless they were seeking forgiveness? *I was drunk, it didn't mean anything.* But Isla knew that was of little comfort to the wronged, even if it were ever true. No, she saw confession as a purely selfish act, to relieve the wrongdoer of their guilt, to set it free, to remove the weight of it pressing on their heart each day.

Yet on the odd occasion, when Isla and Sam argue, or when he flirts with one of her friends for a little too long, there's a reckless part of her that wants to tell him.

She watches him now as he prepares the vegetable stock, adds a tablespoon of olive oil to the pan, and wonders if Ged ever thinks of telling him too.

Sam turns round for a moment, his expression a question, then he turns away again, stirs the stock with slow precision, the tablespoon chiming against the glass jug. Isla stares at his broad back, T-shirt bunched up by the ties of his apron, feels the weight of the silence he carries within him.

'Shall I read you your horoscope?'

He grimaces. 'You know I don't believe all that stuff – but go on, if you must.'

She scrolls up and down the column until she finds Leo.

'It says, "Try to open up to a loved one, discuss past wrongs and let old wounds finally heal. This week is an auspicious time for a new start."'

Is she imagining it or does he flinch?

Isla clears her throat, opens her mouth to speak, has a sudden impulse to tell him about Ged right now. But the words stick to the roof of her mouth like dry communion wafers and she knows she will never confess.

Instead, she jabs at her phone again, the pan sizzling as Sam browns the shallots and garlic. She reads him a story about a pro-lifer who upset a group of students by handing out leaflets at the local school.

'"The leaflet described the unborn baby at different stages of development."'

She presses her hand to her stomach, imagines a heart the size of a poppy seed, tiny indentations where ears would grow, the nubs of arms and legs.

Sam doesn't respond. Isla knows he has never wanted children, and she realises she has read this particular news story aloud to test his reaction. Rightly or wrongly she takes his silence as confirmation that his position hasn't altered, that having a baby wouldn't feature on his list of ways to save a failing marriage. Perhaps they could pick something else off that list instead – adopt a rescue dog or take a once-in-a-lifetime trip.

The pan hisses a little as he adds the rice, stirs it until the grains are coated with oil, pours in a generous glug of wine. He tips the sliced mushrooms into a small omelette pan on the back ring.

Isla types quickly with her middle finger, finds the local job vacancies, sees the advertisement for a development manager at a prominent engineering firm.

'Isn't this the post you were hoping would come up?' She reads the details to him and he nods.

'It would be a great opportunity,' he says, 'but it's a hundred miles away.'

'Well maybe it's time for a fresh start, just like it says in your horoscope?'

She looks up, waiting for an answer, catches a glimpse of

his unease as he turns away. A stone drops to the pit of her stomach, but she stays quiet, browses the property pages, reads the details of the featured houses to herself: *Charming two bed detached cottage with inglenook fireplace and a wealth of other original features. A great bolthole for those with a romantic soul.*

She watches Sam add a little more stock, tip the cooked mushrooms into the pan, stir the rice gently with the wooden spoon that was once her grandma's. Isla notices a glint of silver at the back of his neck; a thin curb chain she's never seen before. Something tightens in her chest.

She taps her screen again, finds today's quick crossword and starts to fill in the clues. When she's typed in all the easy answers she puts her phone down on the table and thinks more carefully about the final few. She reads a couple of them aloud.

'Seven across is "longing", six letters, and the third letter is "s".'

'Desire?'

She nods and types it in. Sam places the wooden spoon on the counter and pours in the last drop of stock, adds grated parmesan.

'What's the next clue?' he asks.

'Avoid something undesirable by luck or skill. Five letters, begins with "c".'

'Cheat.'

Isla glances up and their eyes meet. Sam blushes, then looks away, lifts down two dinner plates from the rack.

She clicks back on the headline news stories, clears her throat, starts to read aloud again; a story about a man recently released from prison after accidentally killing his child. The girl was chasing a ball down their driveway and her father reversed out without seeing her – she was too small to be visible at the side of his car or in his rear view mirror.

In her grief his wife wanted him punished, hired lawyers, pressed the police to find him in some way culpable. In court they said he should have seen the girl in his wing mirror. Angles were considered, sketches produced.

'"But when Mr Freeman was in prison his wife said she regretted her part in ensuring his prosecution, and even though she couldn't bring herself to forgive him she spoke to him several times on the telephone."'

'Would you have forgiven me?' Sam asks.

Isla looks up. 'Of course,' she says, automatically. But they both know it's a lie.

She carries on reading. '"Mr Freeman said he understood why his wife had acted the way she did. He said he would never forgive himself, let alone expect his wife to, yet while in prison he had come to hope she would give their marriage another chance. The prison was a day's travel from Freeman's house, and he knew it would already be dark when he arrived home after his release. He asked his wife to do one simple thing – to leave the porch light on if she was prepared to take him back. When he arrived, the lawn was filled with hurricane lamps and torches, every light in the house was switched on, strings of fairy lights were wrapped around the fence."'

'You wouldn't need to make a special effort here,' Sam says. 'We always have the lights on. This house is as bright as an operating theatre.'

Isla knows he's right. She blinds herself to her fears in a dazzle of bulbs, hates the nights she can't sleep, dreads lying awake in the dark, because the darkness makes everything clearer.

When he hands her the wine she acts on an unexpected

impulse, reaches across to switch on the small table lamp, then gets up and flicks off the main spotlights.

Sam pauses for a moment before he picks up the risotto, but neither of them speak. Isla fills their glasses as he carries the plates over. As she pushes her phone aside, a photograph catches her eye. A man and a woman with their arms around each other's waists, posing for the camera by a backwater canal in Venice. A glimpse of denim sky above the narrow buildings, the water below as dark as moss, a string of sun-bleached washing strung between two balconies. The figures are standing in shadow, some distance from the photographer, yet Isla recognises her friend's gap-toothed grin, the cloud of strawberry hair tied up with a blue scarf.

'Edie's on the local news website! Why is she in Venice?' She peers more closely to see if she knows the man. 'Who on earth is she with?'

Sam drops his plate of risotto onto the table a little too quickly and it clangs against his wine glass. Isla looks up, then back down at the photograph, taking in the short-sleeved shirt patterned with red hibiscus flowers. She reads the paragraph underneath, her hand shaking. She waits until Sam places the second plate of risotto down in front of her, then holds out her phone.

He takes it from her, eyes narrowed; puzzled at first. Then his jaw slackens and he blinks in slow motion as though to clear his vision. Isla watches his mouth half forming the words as he reads, as he tries to work out exactly how this could have happened, as he realises that everything can change irrevocably in the time it takes to make a risotto.

One of our readers found a camera on Lumb Lane in East Cromley last weekend. The camera itself has suffered serious damage, but Mr Harris thought the owner may wish to be reunited with their photographs and suggested we might share one of them here. We checked the memory card and found this romantic snap of a couple in Venice. We'd like to thank Mr Harris, and hope the owner of the camera will see themselves and give us a call.

Sam places the phone down carefully at the side of Isla's plate, picks up his fork as though he plans to eat the risotto, clasps it tightly until the skin over his knuckles is as white as the bone beneath. Then he shrugs, loosens his grip, makes the decision not to fight it.

'I remember now. Edie put her camera down on the roof of the car. We must have forgotten and driven off...'

'Yes, you must have.'

Isla reaches across the table, turns off the lamp with a sharp click. The sound hangs there for a few moments in the darkness as their eyes adjust.

Some Kind of Happy

Livvy and Hugh travelled by ferry from Nice to Calvi and rented a tiny bergerie in the northern mountains of La Balagne. It was high season, and the woman in the tourist office told them they were lucky to find anywhere.

Their only neighbour was the owner of the bergerie, Jean-Luc, who lived in a farmhouse screened by olive trees at the far side of the lane, and who introduced himself with a gift of Corsican wine and a small basket of peaches. He appraised Livvy with his dark eyes and she smiled at him, met his gaze until he looked away.

She was happy to be in Corsica, happy to escape the cosmopolitan chatter of the café life in Nice. Hugh had known several other couples staying at the hotel, and every day they'd eaten a late lunch together on the terrace, drinking wine long into the sleepy afternoons. In the evenings they would stroll along the Promenade des Anglais and drink brandy and coffee in Café Amandine. His friends were always there too – the women slightly drunk and very loud.

She told Hugh she felt more at home here in the mountains, even though she was a city girl at heart. He smiled and stroked her hair, then went back to reading his newspaper. He found it hard to relax, as he loved the company of his friends and was not one for making his own entertainment. During the days he drove Livvy along the narrow mountain roads in his open-top car. She tied back her long hair with a red ribbon, and they went down to the coast for lunch, watched the Italian tourists stroll by in their designer clothes.

And each evening they walked up to the village for an early dinner at Bartoli's, then sat outside the bergerie with their brandy as lizards darted around the lights.

Livvy often lay awake long after Hugh had gone to sleep. She thought about all the men she had ever known, and all the men she would never know if she stayed with Hugh. The men with rough hands and dark eyes, the men with smooth skin and sharp suits, the men who cared nothing for expensive things or vacuous small talk, and the men who cared for little else but money and the sound of their own voices. The men who took her body without offering their love, who placed cash on the bedside cabinet and left without saying goodbye.

She had intended the escort work to be a temporary thing after she lost her job at the insurance office, but it had become easier to continue with it than look for something else. Livvy found it suited her. In fact, if she was honest with herself, she enjoyed it – more than enjoyed it. She loved sex without commitment, that brief connection with something elemental which never failed to make her feel truly alive. She relished the company of men – the way they flirted with her, flattered her, wined and dined her. And she liked the fact that she had the ultimate say in whether or not they came home with her afterwards. She built up relationships with her clients but wasn't tied to one man. She had her freedom and her independence but she wasn't lonely.

All in all, life was good. She had enough money to live well, and a nice apartment in Marylebone. She was happy – not happy in the way the average girl was happy perhaps, but she was some kind of happy – and she told herself it was enough, that she had the best of both worlds.

But when Livvy first met Carl, it made her unsure of her chosen life. In Carl she was sure she'd found her soulmate.

He was charming and generous, passionate about life and the things he believed in. After they made love – which was how she thought of it with Carl – he often brewed them coffee in her kitchen, rustled up a sandwich or an omelette, read out funny stories from the newspaper. And she believed, for that brief hour or two, that this was real life.

Some evenings he stayed longer, fell asleep for a while in her bed. She curled up at his side, rested her head on his chest, waited for him to wake up and tell her about his life, about how much he loved his daughter and why he'd never leave his wife for fear of losing his little girl. Yet Livvy dared to hope that one day he might. She watched him as he slept, his dark hair on the pillow, his arm thrown above his head, and she could almost touch that fantasy world, the world where she and Carl were a couple.

Then, one evening, he took her to a networking event at the Azalea Club, introduced her to everyone as his PA. They both drank too much champagne at the reception, and he ordered a second bottle of wine with the meal. In a drunken moment he told Livvy he wished he was married to her rather than his wife. He said it would make his life so much easier to be with a woman who actually enjoyed sex. Then he threw back his head and laughed, said what was he thinking, that of course she had to appear to enjoy it, she was a sex worker after all. The couple at the next table looked round, smirking, as though they had heard every word, and Livvy stood up, walked calmly towards the cloakroom, collected her jacket and called a cab.

A week later she met Hugh. He took her to a candlelit rooftop restaurant which resembled a Sicilian terrace, held her hand across the table and told her she was too beautiful to be an escort. He was a quiet man, unassuming, the kind of man whose face you would forget five minutes after he left a room. But he was wealthy, lonely, available, and spent most of the year travelling around Europe and staying in beautiful hotels – in the south of France, in Venice, Lake Como, Seville. More importantly, he was kind.

And eight weeks later in their hotel room in Nice, Hugh asked her to marry him, told her she could think about it for as long as she needed to, that he would still want to be with her whatever answer she gave him. And, thought Livvy, he still wanted to be with her despite the fact that she was – as Carl so accurately described her – a sex worker.

Livvy knew he would be a good choice. A wise choice. He was the man who would surely save her from herself; the man who would protect her from what she wanted. A man who knew her past yet hadn't judged her for it. With Hugh there was no need for pretence, no reason to lie, and there would be no prying questions to avoid.

But the decision kept Livvy awake, night after night. It should have been so easy to say yes to him, but part of her was holding back: the part of her that understood how important freedom was; the part of her that knew she wasn't in love with Hugh; the part of her that said she shouldn't marry him simply because she was grateful.

Sometimes she would go out into the garden after he had fallen asleep. She walked barefoot between the trees so she could feel the dry grass brush her skin, and when she reached the edge of the olive grove she waited for the shooting stars to arc across the darkness and wished upon every one.

One afternoon they strolled up to the village earlier than usual. The sun threw long shadows across the deserted main street and they sat alone on the restaurant terrace with their cold beers. As the afternoon turned to dusk, Bartoli lit the pizza oven and four villagers playing petanque asked if Hugh and Livvy would join the final game while they waited for their food. They took their places on opposite teams, and Livvy realised that one of her team was their neighbour, Jean-Luc. He bowed to her, then kissed her hand, and she found herself staring at him again, transfixed by his dark eyes.

The village men pulled another table across and sat with them afterwards, and Bartoli brought out marinara pizzas and jugs of local white wine, lit the candles when dusk fell. He translated the conversation from Corsican into basic French, which Hugh translated into English for Livvy. She drank too much wine and flirted openly, untying her hair and letting it hang loose in a waterfall of ripened wheat. Jean-Luc rested his arm along the back of her chair, and she leaned against it to feel the warmth of his skin.

She looked at the other men – each of them reminding her of someone else: Stefanu, tall and blond, with the smile just like the stockbroker who had taken her out for lunch every Friday; the wiry man in the dark shirt who made her think of the artist from Camden with the disabled wife; Bartoli, whose eyes were the same piercing blue as the accountant who took her out for a Japanese meal once a month, yet never came back to her apartment. All men were the same and all men were different. She watched each of them in turn, imagined taking them to her bed, then reached underneath the table and rested her hand on Jean-Luc's thigh.

When Hugh said it was time to leave, Livvy told him to go back to the bergerie alone. But the track was steep and uneven, hard to negotiate in the dark, and he said he wouldn't go without her, that it wasn't safe for her to walk back on her own. She protested that Jean-Luc would walk down with her later, but Hugh took her by the hand and pulled her to her feet. The village men all cheered and laughed as she staggered down the cobbled street, and she blew kisses at them.

And when she couldn't sleep, Livvy slipped out into the moonlight as she did every night and walked naked to the other side of the garden. She threw her head back, watched the bright blaze of shooting stars high above. And she didn't cry out when two strong arms encircled her from behind, because she knew who it was without turning round. For some reason she had been expecting him, even though he had never followed her out here before. She lay down at the edge of the swimming pool, and though the stone flags were still warm beneath her, she shivered as she looked into his eyes.

Moonlight danced on the pool, and the reflections that ran over their skin made it appear as though they were underwater. As their pale limbs tangled and arced, they rose and fell as one, shooting stars stitching the sky above them with silver thread.

At that moment she was part of the earth, the air, the water and the sky, and Hugh was every man she had ever known. Livvy knew for certain that it would be Hugh who would save her, Hugh who would always protect her from the reckless things she wanted.

The Names of the Missing

Left to her own devices, Kara explored the streets of Berlin alone, avoiding the crowds and seeking out hidden back-streets and alleyways. She took photographs of buskers in full song, street vendors selling falafel and bratwurst, restaurant workers smoking in kitchen doorways, and sometimes – but only with their permission – the homeless.

When Kara and her husband first arrived in the city, the weather was warm and dry, but it had rained intermittently for several days now. She'd been forced indoors to seek out fringe art exhibitions and afternoon concerts, to take long lunches in steamed-up cafés. The sky alternated between pewter and black, water rattled down drainpipes and dripped endlessly from shop awnings.

A group of buskers always played in the same doorway, not far from the apartment where Kara and Stephen were staying: a girl of around eighteen, a middle-aged woman, two men of indeterminate age. Kara took them to be a family and was captivated by their haunting songs. It was music for the soul; rhythms imbued with indefinable yearning; lyrics sung in Arabic, heavy with the weight of loss, the words telling Kara any story she wanted to hear. The faster songs were hypnotic; they brought to mind whirling dervishes, flamenco dancers, Greek *rebetika*. The melodies whipped around inside Kara's head like spinning tops, recalling days filled with sunlight, tables covered with check cloths in the shade of olive trees, a street cat toying idly with a scrap of stale bread, the lulling of gentle waves. She felt a familiar longing for everything lost and forgotten, all those lives dreamed of yet never pursued, a nostalgic pull towards abandoned loves, absent friends, laughter in a distant bar. But all of those things were so long ago now, and when the music slowed down again she thought only of her missing boys.

Kara often stopped to listen to the buskers on her way back to the apartment, dropping coins into the battered tin held out by the girl at the end of each song, exchanging a few words with each of them, asking permission to take pictures. She photographed the girl dancing and the older woman singing, tapping out a beat on the wooden box she used as a stool.

One afternoon, hurrying past them in a sudden downpour, Kara saw the girl run across the road into a coffee shop, hastily tying a bright scarf around her head. Anxious to escape the heavy rain, she followed her inside.

The girl's scarf was spun from lightweight wool, so fine it was almost sheer, patterned with a riot of birds and flowers – peonies in the brightest pinks, lovebirds and parrots against a cobalt blue sky.

'I love your scarf,' she said. 'The colours are beautiful.'

The girl looked Kara up and down before answering. 'It was my mother's scarf – she gave it to me when I left.'

'Isn't that your family?' asked Kara, pointing across the street.

She frowned, shook her head. 'No, they are my friends. My mother and her sister are both missing. They left our village months ago, but no one knows if they made it out of the country.'

'Were they heading here, to Berlin?'

The girl shrugged. 'My mother's phone is answered by a man. A stranger. Many are lost when they leave.' She pointed at the girl behind the counter. 'Alika has a list of people from many places; the names of the missing and the names of the dead. People come here when they have news – leave contact details. My mother's name is on the list. I've heard nothing yet, but I know one day she will come here, just as I know the sunshine will return again.'

The girl turned back to the counter and ordered four coffees. She exchanged words with Alika in Arabic, their expressions momentarily serious, then picked up a cardboard holder containing her coffees and headed towards the door.

Kara thought about the time she and Stephen visited Nagasaki, a year or so before the boys were born, remembered being told about the list of the missing their guide's mother had made on the day the atom bomb destroyed the city.

It had been raining relentlessly on the morning they visited the Peace Park – the exact same weather they were having now in Berlin. When it finally stopped, the smell of slick-wet pavements lingered, and in the crowded tramcar pools of tears formed beneath furled umbrellas. Their guide, Chiyoko, stood at Kara's side as they headed north from the bay, and she remembered thinking that Chiyoko's mother, Harumi, must have made a similar journey on that August morning in 1945 as she travelled to the primary school where she worked. The school was just south-east of the main area of bomb damage, and it became Harumi's job to count and list the surviving children and make a record of those who'd died. Kara remembered Chiyoko's gentle voice, the way she stood, neat and composed, holding on to a quiet sorrow which was never far beneath her smile. It was as though she carried the weight of all those who had lost their lives that day.

Kara was suddenly aware of Alika's voice, asking her what

she wanted to drink. She ordered an espresso, noticed that at the side of the counter there was a clipboard – thick sheets of well-thumbed paper, their edges curling, handwriting in several shades of blue ink, names crossed out and repeated, notes in different scripts and many languages.

'Is that the list of the missing?' she asked.

Alika frowned, tipped her head to one side questioningly. 'What do you know about the list?'

Kara pointed across the street. 'The girl you served just now – with the pretty scarf. She told me about it.'

Alika nodded. 'Do you have information for the list, do you know someone who is searching for family?'

Before she had time to consider it, Kara picked up the pen at the end of the counter. 'I do. That is, I am. Searching I mean. For my two sons.'

'Write their names and ages down on the next page,' she said, 'and any other details. Plus your phone number or email address.' She revealed a fresh sheet of paper, a sheet already embossed with the pen impressions from a dozen full pages above it.

Kara wrote down her phone number, then her boys' names, one underneath the other:

Daniel Halton

Jason Halton

Alika placed two coffees on a tray and handed change to a tall woman who'd been waiting behind Kara in the queue. Then she turned back to her, looked at the names on the list.

'When did they go missing?' she asked. 'And where? How old are they? You need to put these things here.'

Kara picked up the pen again, hesitated for a moment, then wrote underneath their names. *Twins. Missing since January, last seen in north London.*

Alika shook her head. 'January? And London? So why do you think they are now in Berlin?'

'I... well... I heard they'd been seen here.'

Alika looked at her doubtfully, as if she wanted to ask more questions, but in the end she simply nodded. 'Okay, I will ask around. Twins should be easier to spot I think?' She smiled and pushed Kara's coffee across the counter. She handed the girl three euros, picked up the cup and walked over to a free table in the corner.

'Wait,' Alika called. 'You didn't say their ages?'

Kara blushed as heads turned towards her. 'Erm... they would be... twenty now.'

She watched Alika pick up the pen and add their age at the right-hand side.

Kara went back to the coffee shop the following day, and the morning after that, looking at the list each time, checking whether there was anything written next to her boys' names. When she went in on the fourth day it was unusually quiet, and Alika stopped to talk with her for a while.

She told Kara she was at university back home, that she'd been studying medicine alongside her best friend whom she'd known since they were both five years old. Yet now she didn't know where she was, or even if she was still alive.

Kara thought of her friend, Hazel, and the time just after their A levels – that long hot summer when they'd sunbathed in the park, waiting for their lives to begin. Alika may have sat in a park with her best friend too, talking about their clear, bright futures as they watched the birds wash their dusty wings in the fountain, feeling the same knot of excitement and anticipation as Kara did all those years earlier.

But Alika was forced to leave university and set off across

the country with her father when their home and business were bombed. They ended up on a boat which sank close to the Turkish coast and were lucky to reach the shore alive.

'My father and I made it here okay, but not everyone is as fortunate – many many families are left waiting for news. So this is why I decided to list the names of the missing.'

Her gaze was steady as she talked, yet Kara could hear the quiver in her voice. 'And what about your mother?' she asked.

The girl shook her head. 'My mother died when I was just four years old.'

'I'm sorry.'

'And you?' Alika asked, changing the subject. 'Why are you here in Berlin?'

'Stephen – that's my husband – has been seconded here for a couple of months and I decided to come with him.'

'And to look for your boys of course?'

'Yes... yes, of course.'

Alika pulled out a chair and sat down at the table, and for a moment Kara thought she was going to ask more questions about the twins, questions she'd be unable to answer. But when their eyes met, something passed between them, a silent understanding.

'You don't have a job in London?'

'No, not any longer. I haven't worked since my boys... since they went missing.'

Alika put her hand on Kara's wrist. 'You mustn't give up hope. In autumn I may be able to resume my studies at medical school here – a new life for me. And you, you may find your boys. There is always hope.'

Later that day the rain eased off a little, and Kara walked through the Tiergarten, took photographs of the Brandenburg Gate under leaden skies. She had explored every corner of the city over the previous three weeks, walking for miles, always seeing her boys in every face, on every street corner, just as she had seen them in Paris and Rome and Budapest as she drifted in Stephen's wake.

When the showers turned back to heavy rain she looked for shelter in the shops around Unter den Linden. It was there that she saw Alika again, a slender figure in jeans and a dark sweater, a cheap yellow cagoule, her hair tied back with a ribbon. For a brief moment, although she registered her as familiar, Kara was unable to place her when seen out of context, caught up among damp tourists and office workers. Alika was intent on a window display of glorious scarves, patterned with overblown flowers like those painted by the Dutch masters. Kara crossed to stand at her side, and Alika turned and smiled as though she'd been aware of her all along.

'They're lovely,' Kara said. 'As colourful as the scarf your friend wears – the busker.'

Alika nodded, but didn't reply.

'Flowers for the soul,' Kara continued. 'My friend's father was Russian. It was a favourite saying of his: "If I had fifty kopeks, with thirty I would buy bread for my body, and with twenty I would buy lilacs for my soul."'

Alika furrowed her brow, as though she hadn't quite managed to grasp the meaning in English.

'We all need a little beauty in our lives,' Kara said. 'Let me buy the scarf for you?'

She shook her head. 'No, sorry, I cannot allow you to do that. Also, I know you will not find this beauty for your own soul until you find hope. This is what I think you are looking for, Kara, not for missing boys. I must go now, I will be late for my second shift.'

Alika walked away without looking back, her shoulders set, her head held high, and Kara watched the girl disappear into a bright rainbow of anoraks and umbrellas.

Alika wasn't in the café the following day and the manager was on his own behind the counter. Kara ordered a coffee, picked up the clipboard as she waited, saw that someone had written in Arabic at the side of her boys' names.

'Excuse me,' she said, 'do you know what this says?' The man peered at the clipboard and shook his head, shrugged. '*Nein*, I do not speak or read Arabic.'

Kara put the clipboard back, carried her coffee over to the corner table, slopping it into the saucer as she placed it down on the marble surface. She reached inside the inner pocket of her bag to find a tissue, and her hand closed around two neatly folded children's handkerchiefs. She placed them side by side on the table. Both were edged in blue, and in the corner of each was an embroidered initial – a 'J' on one and a 'D' on the other.

She remembered Chiyoko again, her face pressed up to the glass of a display cabinet, pointing out the distorted frame of a small child's tricycle, the remains of broken cups and plates found near ground zero. She talked about the last moments of people's lives at 11.02 that August morning as they started to prepare simple meals in kitchens and cafés across Nagasaki.

'These are the things which matter most,' she said, and stopped to show them a girl's lunch container, the food uneaten, the rice still preserved in the tin.

'I am so sad she did not eat her lunch before she died.' Her eyes filled with tears. 'She would be at her desk, listening to her teacher, perhaps thinking about playing with her friends. And then... and then it happened. The unthinkable.'

Kara remembered her own sadness at seeing the lunch container, the poignancy of a baby's rattle and a twisted, broken wristwatch. She hadn't lost anyone of her own back then, and it was only much later when she realised the real significance of those things, when she understood it wasn't until after someone dies that their possessions become profound – so incredibly profound they can even make a stranger cry. Yet at that same moment those possessions are also rendered pointless. Redundant. Kara thought of her late father's spectacles, her mother's hearing aids, and everything her two boys had ever owned.

Her two boys, killed in the nursery playground by a bus which skidded on ice, careered off the road, smashed through the railings. Dying together, without her, on January 21st 1998. They would be twenty years old now if they were still alive.

She stood up and went over to the counter, intending to cross their names off the list. Daniel Halton. Jason Halton. The names of two boys who would never be coming back.

She picked up the clipboard and started to turn the pages. The manager was watching her from behind the counter. 'Where is Alika today?' she asked.

'She is with her friend.' Suddenly animated, he pointed across the street to where the buskers normally played. 'You know Alika's friend I think? It is good news – her mother has been found, here in Germany. They celebrate!'

As Kara looked across the street, the sun came out again. She put down the list and went back to her table, drank her espresso in a single gulp, suddenly anxious to be outside.

There were maple trees lining the pavement, their tight green buds beginning to unfurl; the promise of new life.

When they'd left the Peace Park in Nagasaki that day, Chiyoko had walked ahead, leading them to two ancient camphor trees at the Sannō Shrine. She touched them fondly, as though they were old friends.

'They are survivors. They have witnessed all that has happened here for the last eight hundred years.'

She told them the story of how the trees had become a symbol of destruction and recovery. In 1945 they were charred and blackened, stripped bare of their leaves by the bomb's shock wave, and yet, despite everything, they remained not only standing, but thriving. She pointed out a fledgling shoot growing from one of the giant trunks. 'This is hope,' she said. And when Chiyoko smiled, something of her sadness finally lifted.

Kara stopped for a moment on the quiet Berlin street, a street where those who had lost everything still managed to find hope. A door banged behind her and the café manager came out, holding up her two initialled handkerchiefs. '*Entschuldigen!* Did you forget these?'

She shook her head and started to walk away as she answered him. 'When you see Alika, could you please tell her I have found my missing boys.'

Something in the Night

As we cross the park, I notice there is a full moon rising, pale as milk. I stumble over a tree root and Keizo catches my hand in his own strong, square one. Paper lanterns stretch ahead of us in the soft dusk: amber, turquoise, red and green, swaying softly in a curving line. When we reach the riverbank it becomes more crowded. Families have spread their rugs out on the grass, and under the strings of fairy lights I can see their smiling faces, the glint of beer glasses. Further along the river there is a row of brightly lit *yatai*, food stalls selling fragrant yakitori meat skewers, succulent octopus balls, chargrilled corn on the cob, mounds of yakisoba noodles.

There is a soft buzz of anticipation. Children dressed in anime costumes and character masks run between the trees, occasionally called back by their anxious mothers – some wearing colourful Noh-style masks of their own. Teenage girls dressed in vivid kimonos giggle together as they stroll along the bank, holding trays of outsize French fries smothered in sauce.

I want to stop here on the periphery of it all, taking it in, inhaling the magic, Keizo's warm hand in mine. For these few precious moments I'm reminded of the things I love about Japan and why I first wanted to come here to teach. I remember the arrivals hall at Narita airport, the fug of my jet lag already kicking in despite the adrenaline and excitement. And just like now, I wanted to stop there a short while, to sit down on a bench and let the world rush past me, hardly daring to catch the train to Tokyo for fear of breaking the spell. At that moment the next chapter of my life was still waiting for me, full of precious gifts, and I could hardly bear it.

'Come on, Anna.'

Keizo tugs at my hand, sets off to search for his friends by the stone bridge where he has arranged to meet them. I am suddenly nervous. He has so many friends and he is anxious for me to like each and every one, eagerly asking for my opinion of them as soon as they have left. When he first introduces me, he always stands at my back, his broad hands resting on my shoulders, as though I am a shy child who needs gentle encouragement. He never seems to notice their reaction to me, yet I am usually unsure whether they like me or not. Often they appear to resent my presence, though it never feels personal. I can hear their internal sighs, see the slight trepidation in their careful expressions, and I understand that it's simply too hard work for them to speak English all the time. They assume I won't understand Japanese, therefore it surely follows that I will somehow hamper their fun, make them feel they must behave a certain way.

Keizo lets go of my hand as he walks over to them, and I notice they are all dressed similarly in dark jeans and T-shirts. When they turn I see they're wearing traditional kitsune fox masks – not the ones I'm used to seeing for sale at festivals, reminiscent of Venetian carnival masks and made from thin plastic, but full masks which cover their entire faces. They look homemade, more substantial, crafted from papier-mâché or light wood.

The group greet Keizo effusively, and a tall girl with shoulder length hair comes forward, reaches in her bag and produces two similar fox faces, hand-painted and decorated with red feathers. They each lift up their masks for a second as they introduce themselves, but as soon as they let them snap back into place I lose my grasp of their features. Their names: Hatsumo, Hiroshi, Michiro, Megumi – and a fifth I don't even catch – are quickly confused and forgotten.

Keizo hands me the smaller of the two papier-mâché masks, so much lighter than anticipated, and I slip the elastic over my head, adjust it so I can see, feel suddenly released from the responsibility of constantly smiling, of pretending to understand the fast-paced Japanese conversation. My new vulpine face renders me anonymous, allows me to become a spectator.

We sit down in a circle, and one of Keizo's friends – the man who introduced himself as Hiroshi as far as I can tell – produces beers from a cool box, while another opens a large plastic bottle of supermarket whisky.

Music plays through loudspeakers along the bank, occasionally interspersed with muffled announcements which I don't even try to decipher. When the fireworks are announced, everyone moves out from beneath the trees to obtain a better view. I stagger a little as I stand – the neat whisky has gone straight to my head – and walk over to watch the show from the centre of the bridge with the others.

When the display begins, the sky splutters to life, suddenly filled with huge, glittering chrysanthemums of light – red and gold and violet. When I look across at Keizo and his friends, I notice the dazzle has turned each mask a silvery blue, has rendered them strangely unsettling, every pair of eyes blank-black, faces turned up to the night sky – a skulk of stargazing foxes.

I remember the book about Japanese spirits which Keizo gave me to read, yet although I know kitsune are the benevolent messengers of Inari, all I can think about is their more mischievous and malevolent side, their ability to shape-shift. In medieval Japan, many believed that every woman out alone after dark was a kitsune, that hidden within her kimono were her many foxtails, as dark as rust beneath the canopy of the forest, or as bright as blood beneath the full moon. There were stories of vixens who became human every evening when they went to their husbands' beds, only to turn back to their vulpine selves come dawn, sometimes killed by packs of village dogs.

When the fireworks are over, a collective sigh of appreciation carries across the water, and Keizo's friends stroll over to the *yatai* to buy yakitori skewers. I hesitate, hang back to watch several couples as they cross the bridge to the other side of the river, hand in hand, disappearing without a word into the trees. Keizo sees me staring at them.

'They are taking the opportunity for time alone in the forest – privacy is hard to come by in the city.'

I am momentarily shocked – it feels like something only teenagers or illicit lovers would do – yet at the same time it also feels exciting. I met Keizo six months ago at the school where we both work, and as he has his own apartment we have never made love elsewhere. I used to ask him if we could visit a love hotel – to assuage my curiosity – but Keizo kept dismissing my requests with excuses, surprisingly coy and embarrassed every time I mentioned them.

I'm suddenly a little jealous of the lovers beneath the trees. I imagine the earthy scent of the warm leaf mould on the forest floor and the gleam of moonlight on silvery leaves. I recall a shiver of anticipation, the almost unbearable wait, the burn of unfulfilled desire, remember the exhilarating joy of warm evening air on naked skin, the static shock of that first touch. I visualise fingers tracing lines across moon-pale stomachs and breasts, slipping down between welcoming thighs. And I ache for that reconnection with the natural world, for the way our primeval carnal acts become something purer when conjoined with the elements. Most of all, I yearn for the frisson of danger, the delicious fear of being caught, of being seen.

I catch Keizo's hand and pull him across the bridge towards the trees, look back questioningly when I feel his reluctance. 'Come on, it will be fun!'

'People have been stolen by spirits in these trees,' he replies.

He sounds serious, but I laugh and tug at his hand again. I can't see his eyes or he mine, but I feel his hand relax.

'Okay,' he says, 'but let's keep our masks on in case there's anyone around from the school.'

I'm sure he's being unnecessarily cautious, but I agree anyway, and he guides me away from the direction in which the other couples have gone and through a gap between two larch trees.

We walk further into the dense foliage, stumble upon an unexpected space surrounded by thick bushes. Keizo spreads out his jacket on the ground and I unfold the thin raincoat I keep in my bag. I sit down, but he doesn't join me straight away, tells me to wait for him there because he needs to pee. In the darkness of the forest his body is camouflaged and all I can make out is his mask, glowing coldly in the moonlight. I hear the crack of a twig, someone laughing in the distance, something move in the branches above my head, Keizo's footsteps as he walks a few yards away from me. Then the forest falls silent.

The colours of the trees have dissolved into a haze of grey branches, leaves and shadows. Inexplicably, I find myself filled with the same sense of dread which envelops me if I wake in the night at Keizo's apartment. There is always a moment before I remember where I am, the grey room reels and spins around me, and the air appears as thick as smoke. It is then, at the edge of time, in that no man's land between night and day, when I truly feel I am an imposter, an alien, an unwanted stranger in an unfamiliar space, drifting above the bed, above Keizo, wondering why I'm here, if I'll ever truly connect or feel at home.

I want to speak to Keizo, to wake him, to make him solid again, to reassure myself he is living and breathing. But I never do. I hold his name gently in my mouth, never letting it slip out between my lips. I try to reassure myself that there will always be something else, something special, within the four walls of his room, something in the night which is softer than the city outside. I reach for his hand beneath the sheet, entwine my fingers with his long, square-tipped ones and fall back to sleep.

I hear his footsteps returning now through the trees, watch him walk towards me, eyes glinting behind the painted mask. Yet although this human form appears to be Keizo, I discover it is possible to believe it is him while knowing that it isn't, to desire both of these things at once; to want the man who is Keizo and the man who isn't. His body is semi-opaque; it is solid, yet fluid, a part of the otherness of the night. Yet the forest has become immense around us, loudening again, and my ears are tuned to the quiver of every leaf, to the footsteps of each tiny creature, to the soft breath of sleeping birds.

The man who both is and isn't Keizo doesn't say a word, simply kneels down in front of me, his familiar hands unfastening the buttons of my shirt. I reach for his mask, but he shakes his head, still silent. I play the game, pick up my own mask again and fasten it over my face. I remember that kitsune spirits have to cover their heads with a handful of greenery, reeds, or even an animal skull, in order to change form. I pluck a handful of pale leaves from a sapling and ceremoniously place them on top of both our heads. He laughs, a small growl of a sound, presses me gently down to the ground. I shiver as the cold leaves fall onto my burning skin, and I inhale the essence of him as he lies down at my side, relish the strange new scent of him, the way I can almost taste the earth, the bark, the sweet petals of woodland flowers, the smokiness of his hair. His movements are different too – more urgent – his fingers probing and demanding.

Separated by the masks, we do not kiss, but our eyes lock. Then I reach for him – this stranger, this dog-fox of the forest, this man who I know is not Keizo – and fumble to unfasten his jeans. As I slide my fingers beneath the waistband, he springs back up, rests on his haunches like a wild creature preparing to pounce, slips his T-shirt over his head, then stands up to finish undressing. He is ghostly, insubstantial, yet his presence all-consuming, He pulls me up with one hand and turns me towards the tree behind him, covers my splayed hands with his own. I can feel his animal breath on my neck, and I arch my back towards him, the scent of him now overpowering: dank, sour, rich, sweet, salt and ozone, decay and freshly cut grass.

When he is inside me I know the truth beyond all doubt, yet I don't care. I want nothing more than this, to reconnect to the earth and the sky, to be consumed by the rustle and quiver of the forest, to belong to something in the night.

I hear Keizo's voice calling me, bewildered to find myself lying down on my raincoat, exactly where I was when he first left me. He is holding the fox mask in his hand now, apologising for how long he's been away.

'I was lost in the trees, even though I thought I'd only walked a short distance. It was confusing – going round in circles! You look as though you've been asleep – you have bits of the forest in your hair. Maybe the whisky went to your head?'

I start to protest, but he laughs at me, ruffles my hair to dislodge the leaves and twigs, then laughs to himself about his own foolishness again, pulls me to my feet, says we'd better be getting back.

'This was perhaps a bad idea after all – Hiroshi-chan will come to look for us if we do not leave soon.'

I feel suddenly exposed, the air cooler on my skin. I slip on my raincoat as we emerge from the trees, mutter something to Keizo about how it feels like rain. We quickly find the others, all walk together through the park to the train station, Keizo's friends teasing him about where we've been, glancing across at me now and again to see if I am following their fast-paced chatter.

In the crowded train everything snaps back into colour – purple and navy T-shirts, red training shoes, a dark green jumper tied around Megumi's shoulders. We stand together, crushed close in the busy carriage. No one talks – everyone seems tired and subdued – and I am relieved not to be drawn into conversation, certain that I look different now, sure that I must appear irrevocably altered.

I can see each of them clearly for the first time and I examine their faces in the bright light. The man whose name I didn't catch is standing closest to me, and I notice how beautiful he is: the thickness of his hair, the taut muscles of his forearms, something animal in his eyes, his pupils almost vertical slits. My eyes travel up to look at his hand holding the overhead strap. I glance away for a moment, blushing, confused, when I see he has the same broad, square-tipped fingers as Keizo. He sees me watching him and he smiles, presses his hip bone into mine as the train sways. His discreet touch is barely perceptible, a single fingertip pressed to the base of my spine at the exact place where my new tail is hidden beneath my coat.

Swimming to the Other Side

'Alice! I'm so relieved you've arrived safely, I've been going out of my mind with worry. Come over here and give your daft old father a kiss. We've heard a lot of gunfire and fighting in the last few days, and children screaming. This morning Margaret told me the Earl has fallen ill. And the food shortages are getting worse. Is there anyone still living in those houses down the hill?'

'Down the hill? You mean towards the village? Well, yes, of course there is.'

'Oh that's good. The staff say that as long as we're still here at the big house then the village will try and help us. But if you could find some food and bring it back up here, then it would really help. We're all quite scared.'

'I'll see what I can find. Look, your lunch is here now – it's salmon. I think you might be exaggerating the food shortages, there's no need to worry.'

'Mmm, that's tasty. Oh I do feel better now you're here – you're so brave Alice. We had to share beds last night to save on heating, and I slept with my friend Elizabeth. But when I woke in the night she'd gone – I don't know where to. It seems odd that the Earl has been throwing parties with all this going on. But he has – I hear them laughing and dancing until well into the night. I've listened to the news, or tried to, but they only talk the local language and my French isn't up to it. My memory's going and I've forgotten the vocabulary.'

'Shush... eat your lunch before it gets cold. I'll be back in an hour.'

'Oh, and Alice, before I forget to tell you, they say four of the girls downstairs are pregnant – all to the same man. And it's him – the Earl! Can you do anything to help them?'

'Wake up, Dad, I'm back. I've brought you some Jaffa Cakes and Cadbury's Mini Rolls. They'll keep you going if you get worried about food shortages.'

'Oh, poppet, you are good to me. What country are we in?'

'England of course.'

'Oh… yes… England…'

'Your hair looks neat this week – has the hairdresser been?'

'Yes… no, I think I went out to see the barber. 2/6d it costs now, I can't afford to go very often. What's the name of this place again? Don't roll your eyes, Alice – you forget the names of things as you get older. Just you wait until it happens to you!'

'This is Beeches Nursing Home, Dad.'

'What does your mother think about the civil war then?'

'She died, remember?'

'Oh yes, I'd forgotten about that. Am I confused?'

'Yes, I think you might be a little confused today.'

'Put *Doc Martin* on then will you, there's a love? ITV3.'

'Alice? Is it really you? I'm so glad to see you! Do they know you're here downstairs? Have they seen that you're alive?'

'Alive? What do you mean? I've been here hours. You nodded off in the middle of your TV programme – *Doc Martin* – remember? Dad, why are you crying, what's the matter?'

'*Doc Martin*? I don't know what you mean. Is he the doctor that said you'd been murdered? I haven't been eating since they said you'd been killed. Do you know who they said had murdered you? Me! With John's help. Can you believe it?

Why didn't they tell me that you were alive? The coroner should have told me. It's very bad form. I've been so upset…'

'Dad, I'm fine, you must've had a bad dream. It's all these detective shows you watch.'

'Now even you don't believe me. It's not a dream, it's true. I saw it on the news. What am I going to do if you aren't on my side any more? It's like when I was in hospital and we had to dress up to be on that Jeremy Kyle's show. You wouldn't bring me my best suit. And you never believe me when I tell you about the nurses and what they make us do. They fire us down a chute into the river and we have to swim to the other side and then get out on the far bank. But it's patrolled by fierce guard dogs, so when we get out we have to run. I can't see me ever managing that. But we won't be allowed home from hospital unless we do it. I can't understand why you don't believe me…'

'Dad, it's okay, I know you're not making things up.'

'Well then, who was really murdered if it wasn't you? Why won't you tell me? What does your mother think? You're living with her now, so she must've known what was going on. She hasn't been to visit me even though we've been married sixty-five years.'

'Dad, don't you remember? Mum died.'

'Oh yes, I forgot about that. There's nothing good about ageing you know.'

'Would you like me to ask them to make you a cup of tea? You could have a Mini Roll.'

'Yes, that'd be lovely. I do like a nice Mini Roll – as long as they're Cadbury's ones of course. I can't see the television you know. It's all a blur. And they speak French. And in the night they turn that thing on above the bed and wake you up with a cold shower, just as you're getting cosy.'

'That's a light fitting, Dad, not a shower. Look, I'm turning it on and off. It's a light fitting.'

'It's a shower. I don't know why you don't believe me. And when they dress you afterwards they ruin all your clothes. They just yank them hard over your head. It stretches the necks. All my best jumpers are ruined.'

'There's a letter here from Frank, shall I read it to you?'

'Yes please.'

'He says he hopes you're improving after the stroke, and that he'll come and see you as soon as he's feeling a bit better himself. He says he's had a lot of trouble with his breathing, and he's been in and out of hospital.'

'Yes, well, we're all getting older, and it's no fun. Frank's such a lovely man.'

'He is, isn't he. I hope he'll get to see you soon. Has Jean been to visit you?'

'No.'

'Well her name's in the visitor book from yesterday.'

'No. She never comes. Though I do forget things these days. I'm sorry I haven't got you an Easter egg. I don't get out much now you know.'

'Well you look after yourself, and I'll see you again tomorrow. Don't cry, Dad...'

'Alice, it's Margaret here from the Beeches. I'm sorry, but I've got bad news. Your dad passed away early this morning. It was very peaceful. The doctor said he had another stroke in his sleep and he wouldn't have known anything about it.'

'Okay, Margaret, I'll come straight over. I'm relieved the ending was gentle.'

'I think he sensed it somehow, because last night when I put him to bed he asked me to tell you something – it was as though he didn't expect to see you again.'

'What did he say?'

'Well it was quite funny, and it doesn't seem appropriate when I've only just given you such sad news.'

'No, go ahead and tell me, Margaret, it's fine.'

'He started saying "Tell Alice I've done it!" over and over again. I kept asking him what he'd done. He said "I went down the slide into the river and I managed to swim to the other side. And then I raced along the bank and the dogs didn't catch me – I outran them! I'm going home to Alice's mother tonight, so I won't be here when she comes tomorrow. You'll tell her, won't you?" And then he… Alice, are you still there? Alice? I knew I shouldn't have told you this now. Are you okay?'

'I'm still here, Margaret. And yes, I'm okay. In fact, it's the perfect ending.'

In Felicity's World

On Friday lunchtime Felicity took a thick marker pen from the stationery cupboard and started writing in her desk diary. She spoke the words aloud as she scrawled *PATRICK MOVING IN* in large black capitals. She wrote it across the entire weekend. Loud and clear.

She'd used a calendar the previous year. However, the only place to hang it was at the back of her desk where she couldn't be sure it would reach her target audience. So this year she'd bought a desk diary. A large, expensive, red leather desk diary. A diary you couldn't help noticing. She always left it open at the current week, the weighted ribbon holding down the smooth cream pages.

Not that anyone ever needed to walk past her desk. For some reason they had all moved their own desks to the other end of the office. They said something about the sun shining onto their computer screens. It didn't really matter, as the diary was mainly for Patrick's benefit rather than theirs. She decided some time ago that he needed to understand just how popular she was, how much in demand. Consequently, anyone who cared to look would see that Felicity often had lunch with the girls, visited the theatre with Chris, and had been invited to Teresa's for a weekend in the country. And occasionally there would be the odd retrospective note about a fabulous dinner or a brilliant film.

But this was the big event of the year so far – in fact the biggest event in Felicity's life for some time. It was the weekend when Patrick would be moving in.

She'd given him the ultimatum when he broke a date with her to attend Julia's surprise birthday party. Three and a half years she had waited. Now it was was finally time for him to leave Julia and move in with her. Then they could announce their relationship to the world and go out together in public. And she would make sure he stayed with her for good. She had a book: *Ten Essential Rules for Trapping a Man and Keeping Him*. Even Felicity had to admit there was room for improvement in her skills when it came to keeping them.

On Thursday afternoon Patrick had disappeared on a short business trip. He told Felicity not to call him as he would be with clients until late in the evening, followed by a business breakfast on Friday morning. For once she'd done as she was told – although she had sent him a quick text earlier saying she couldn't wait to see him the next day. She was confident that didn't really count.

She pushed her diary to the front of the desk and glanced across at the others. There had been a strange atmosphere in the office all day and everyone kept looking at her rather oddly. She wondered if they'd overheard her and Patrick talking. Some of the girls had worked with him for years, and they knew Julia as well. None of them really approved. But she didn't care what they thought.

As she walked home she planned everything she needed to do before Patrick arrived the next day. She would wax her bikini line, paint her nails and blow dry her hair, and tomorrow she would go to the supermarket for champagne and something special for their supper.

In the morning a wedding car passed her as she walked into town, bedecked with ribbons, obviously on its way to pick up a bride. She smiled to herself. It was a sunny day, Patrick would be with her later, and one day soon she too would be driving to church in a white Rolls Royce. So what if she was pushing forty, Felicity would have the dress she had always wanted. She had never doubted he would leave Julia, despite what Andrea in accounts said. After all, they'd never married, and he wouldn't have started seeing Felicity unless he'd planned to be with her in the end. It was obvious, and why Andrea couldn't see it she had no idea. But then again, she was probably jealous. It was clear that all the women at Parker Routledge fancied Patrick.

She called him as she walked around Tesco. His phone went straight to messages, but she took it as a good sign. Patrick never switched his phone off even when he was at home with Julia, because he was on call 24/7 for work. That meant he must have told her and they were arguing. She was probably pleading with him to stay as he packed his case.

Felicity had made a small space in her wardrobe. He wouldn't have much stuff after all. He had lived with Julia for seven years, but it was her house, so he would only have his clothes and a few bits and pieces. He had a dog called Poppy, but she would have to lay the law down there. No dogs allowed. It was an elderly terrier and it was bound to smell – and yap.

She hoped he wouldn't bring too many clothes. She didn't want clutter everywhere. Patrick liked clothes. He wore soft wool suits, Italian loafers and solid gold cufflinks. He was always tanned and his hair was strawberry blond. Well actually it was grey, but he went to the hairdresser every few weeks to have it dyed. Sometimes it came out a muddy brown colour in patches at the back. He teased it up into spikes to hide the fact that it was thinning.

Felicity's own hair was dark and sleek, an immaculate

helmet like Anna Wintour's. She had no clue what Julia's hair was like. She had never seen her, not even in a photograph. Keeping her faceless helped Felicity to control the annoyance she felt. She knew what she would be like anyway – faded and grey, frumpy and nondescript.

As she paced the supermarket aisles, she imagined Patrick arriving. He would lift her up onto the kitchen worktop, kiss her gently and hand her a bouquet of flowers. And she wouldn't have to check with him whether he'd bought Julia a bunch too, or ask whose had cost the most. Not that he would tell her. Patrick was a secretive man. He always answered a question with another question, and never gave his opinion on anything until he knew what the other person was thinking.

And actually, flowers were unlikely. He rarely bought her presents. And when he did it was always something impersonal, like a bottle of gin charged to expenses at the airport duty free shop. Felicity suspected he might be a little tight with his money, but it didn't matter, so was she. She put the champagne back and selected a bottle of cava instead.

Saturday afternoon passed slowly. Every so often she picked up the phone to make sure it was still working and checked her mobile for text messages. Maybe Julia was causing more of a scene than Patrick had expected. Every time she heard a car she went to the window to see if it was his. He didn't normally park down her lane, he always hid the car around the corner, but from now on he could park right outside.

At seven o'clock she called his mobile again. It was still switched off. Angrily, she called his home number. It rang and rang.

At nine o'clock Felicity put the salmon steaks back in the fridge and opened the bottle of cava. She had tried his home number seventeen times, but there was still no answer. She left an angry message on his mobile, then a second one with a grudging apology.

She searched through the television channels. There was a rerun of *Fatal Attraction*. She flicked over again. She hated that film, she had never understood why anyone would chase after a man like that. Where was the woman's pride? Let the men do the chasing, that's what Felicity always maintained. And that's what *Ten Essential Rules* advised too.

After she finished the wine she fell asleep in the chair, waking with a start at the sound of gunshots on the television. She checked her watch – midnight. Reluctantly she went up to bed. Patrick was probably waiting for Julia to fall asleep. Anyway, he had a key to get in if he arrived later.

Felicity slept in on Sunday, and when she finally got up she felt groggy from drinking the whole bottle of cava. She checked her phones for messages again – nothing. Obviously something must have kept him. Possibly Julia had forced him to spend another day with her. They went to her mother's every Sunday for lunch and it would be difficult to cancel at such short notice without an explanation. Julia would need to save face.

Felicity tried to shrug it off. He could fetch his things straight after work on Monday and the salmon would still be fine for their supper.

She went to work in her favourite dress the next morning, humming softly to herself. Patrick was always in before her, but today he wasn't at his desk. She went to find Andrea to see if she knew where he was. Andrea looked at her in that odd way she sometimes did. It was almost as though she pitied her. It was an emotion which didn't exist in Felicity's world; an emotion she didn't really understand. It reminded her of Barry in the drawing office when his dog died. He had cried at work and everyone fussed around him as if they cared. The boss had actually let him go home. Imagine crying over a stupid dog.

'Patrick's on holiday this week, didn't you know?' said Andrea. Felicity pretended she'd forgotten and strolled back to her office in a show of indifference. So that was why they had all looked at her like that on Friday. Julia had made Patrick go on one of her last minute holidays to Tenerife, or wherever it was they went. As usual he hadn't dared tell her. Felicity and Patrick always fell out when he went on holiday. She hated the thought of him spending so much time with Julia. However, she always used the time wisely while he was away. A workout every day in the gym, a haircut, a pedicure, and then she made sure she wore her best dress on the Monday morning when he was due back. And that's what she would do this time as well. She felt her anger dissolve as her plan formed. After all, it wasn't Patrick's fault that Julia had sprung this on him just as he was planning to leave her. Felicity feigned a bad period pain and went home.

By Saturday morning she felt much better. She had survived the week at work without him, and now there was just the weekend to get through and he would be hers.

She grabbed the local paper from the mat to read over breakfast, turning straight to her favourite page – the wedding write-ups. She loved to imagine the day her own wedding photo would be in there. The whole of Parker Routledge would see that Patrick loved her, not Julia. She examined the photos closely, appraising the dresses and hairstyles.

Then her heart stopped. For a moment it was silent in Felicity's world except for the ticking of the clock.

Now she knew what Julia looked like. She was a little younger than Felicity had imagined, blonde and pretty, self-assured, kind eyes and an open smile. She had a single flower in her hair and wore an elegant ivory dress. Patrick stood at her side in a pale linen suit, looking as happy as she had ever seen him. Underneath the photograph she read: *The couple were married at the register office, before departing the following day for a week's honeymoon on the Amalfi coast.*

She fetched the kitchen scissors and cut out the photo, propped it up against the coffee pot, memorised every detail. It was certainly a setback, and it would be a little harder for him to leave Julia now she had tricked him into marriage, but Felicity didn't see it as a serious problem. She took her empty coffee cup over to the sink, then picked up a bowl and ran some hot water to start her pedicure. She had just two days left before he got back from his honeymoon.

About Life

I lie still, not wanting to wake you – yet wondering if you are already awake and thinking the same. I listen to your breathing and watch you in the half-light, note the curve of your back, tangled hair the dusty yellow of a lion's belly. There is something vulnerable about you in sleep, almost childlike, and I feel a rush of affection, another flash of desire. Part of me hopes you'll stay, drink coffee with me, say yes when I ask if you'd like eggs and toast. You drove us home last night – you said you'd only had two beers – and part of me hopes you'll suggest a drive to the coast, lunch in a village pub, or even just a walk down to the park.

Yet another part of me isn't sure whether I want to speak to you at all, whether it would be better to feign sleep, lie silent, eyes closed, while you get dressed and leave. That part of me knows I am too recently damaged to start a relationship with you, to keep up any pretence of being "normal", that it's for the best if I let you go, that it is too soon for me to trust another man.

But a final part of me hopes that if you leave now you'll write your number on the pad in the kitchen, a short note saying what a lovely evening you had, that you'll call me later. So, yes, if I'm honest with myself, I know for certain I don't want you to leave without a note or a word, without some clear idea of whether there will be a "you and me".

I'd seen you in the nightclub a few times – well you know that, because I told you almost straight away. I'd willed you to look at me, to make eye contact, to walk across the room and take my arm, to steer me by the elbow towards the empty booth in the corner. But your eyes always skimmed past me, unfocused, as you talked to your friend, gesticulating with your bottle of beer as you chatted and laughed, oblivious to everyone else in the room.

In the end I followed you to the bar, squeezed in at your side, bumped against you and caused you to spill your beer onto my wrist. You apologised profusely despite the fault being mine, even offered to pay for my wine. And then, just like that, you were mine. You didn't even ask those usual awkward questions about why I was alone in the club, and so there were no lies to tell you about friends who'd left me in the lurch. It was that easy in the end.

You turn over onto your back and I quickly close my eyes. Then you sit up in bed, reach behind you to pull the curtain aside, let a thick wedge of winter sunlight flood the room. I murmur and open my eyes, pretend you've woken me.

You smile and reach for your phone. 'Shit. Nine o'clock already? Mam and Brian will kill me. I can't believe I didn't wake up earlier.'

You jump up and start dressing without further explanation, and I know you're doing a runner on me. "Mam and Brian" for Christ's sake?

'Can I make you a coffee?' I ask, still hoping for something more.

You shake your head, pull on your jumper, and wander through to the living room to find your shoes. 'I'm really sorry, Joanna,' you shout, 'but I really have to go. Give me your number and I'll call you later.'

You come back into the bedroom, phone in hand, and I pull the sheet up to my chin. 'You don't need to say that if you don't want to call.'

I smile after I say it, as though it's unimportant to me, but my heart is hammering. You called me by my name. I'm a person again, an individual, suddenly visible after being so long in the dark.

You walk over to me, kiss the top of my head. Then you glance at the clock on my bedside cabinet.

'How quickly can you get dressed?' you ask. 'No fancy stuff – just a pair of jeans, some sturdy boots, a warm coat?'

'Where are we going?'

'You'll see when we get there. I have to work, but you can come with me if you want – I'd really like you to.'

As we drive to your mother's farm you tell me you are ploughing today, that you'd promised to help them this weekend, as your stepfather has injured his back. We pass fields still striped with snow in every ridge, reluctant to thaw in the late winter sunlight.

When we arrive, you take out overalls and a tweed cap from the boot of the car. You look at my boots doubtfully and fetch a pair of wellingtons from the porch – your mother's, a size too big – and I sit on the fence halfway up the field to watch you plough. The first new furrows stretch away towards the cliff edge, dark and loamy.

I wave as you drive past me, but the sun reflects off the tractor windscreen and I can't tell if you wave back. You reach the end of the field and turn. Now you have your back to me, your blond hair curling out from under the cap.

I think about the size and weight of the tractor, the fact that – if I chose to – I could throw myself underneath it at the last moment. I imagine the wheels forcing the breath out of me, pressing me down into the damp earth.

Your mother appears at the gate, walks up to where I'm

sitting and hands me a bag. 'Some sandwiches for you both,' she says, 'and a flask of tea. I can't hang about, there's the chickens to sort out and a calf to check on in the bottom field.' Then, as she turns to go, she says something else. 'He doesn't often bring anyone here, our Andy. I guess I'll be seeing you again then, Joanna.'

My heart somersaults. She said my name too. I feel warm inside as I watch her walk away, then I stride out across the field, kicking up the dark soil, waiting impatiently for you to come back down again.

You are heading towards me now, and you wave, smiling. I hold up the lunch bag. You carry on to the end of the field, complete the new furrows before you stop, then jump down from the cab and walk over to me. I pour a cup of tea from the flask and hand you one of the sandwiches. You bite into the thick bread and gulp the tea down in one.

'I have to get back to it, I'm sorry,' you say. You kiss me on the forehead. I nod, watch you walk back to the tractor, leap up in one easy stride.

I sit on the gate in the corner and eat the other sandwich, then cup both hands around my tea. I'd half hoped you'd stay and talk, but I understand why you can't, that you need to keep going. And strangely, it's enough just to be here with you. Despite the cold, I don't move, I watch you driving up and down the field, turning the earth, the seagulls swooping and diving overhead.

And although I know farming is as much about death as it is about birth, right now, everything happening here in front of me is about life. Ploughing, planting, tending new-born calves, tiny chicks shuddering out into the world from within fragile shells. Everything feels different here, today, away from the prison of my own thoughts. I suddenly know that I'm ready for my life to restart.

I set off across the field before I can change my mind. I ache to hear you call me by my name again, need to hear you say it – an affirmation that I am here, that I am alive. The tractor moves steadily towards me and I can see your face clearly. I run to you then, waving for you to stop, but catch my foot on the edge of a furrow and stumble. There is a flash of fear in your eyes. You swerve, there's a judder as the tyre glances my shoulder, and I lurch back, throwing myself to the ground. The engine cuts out, and for a moment there is only the murmur of the radio. Then I hear you clambering down, stumbling in your haste, shouting my name.

Something In, Something Out

Carleen leans heavily on the counter, drums her bitten fingernails on the scratched laminate as she waits for Jodie to finish explaining the new shift pattern. Then she pushes her hair behind her ear, smooths down her skirt and walks out across the red tiled floor, a coffee jug held out like communion wine.

Doug watches her from the kitchen hatch. He knows only an unwary out-of-towner will dare to catch her eye and ask for a refill. The regular customers have seen her mood of late, have practised feigning disinterest, know to wait until she comes to them, and to meet her tired smile with a silent nod as they slide their cup across to the edge of the table. Carleen circles the room just once, avoiding eye contact, then places her jug back on the counter top. She turns back to stack a pile of empty plates, then carries them over to the hatch.

'What's biting you today, Carleen?' Doug asks as he takes the crockery over to the dishwasher. Though why he bothers to enquire he's no longer sure. He likes her well enough, perhaps more than he cares to admit, but since her no-good man upped and left a couple of months back he can't seem to get any sense out of her.

Carleen ignores him and slides back behind the counter. She's always had a soft spot for Doug, though she's taken care to hide it. He has kind eyes and a good word to say about everyone. But whenever she talks to him he makes it awkward by asking her to go to the bowling alley or the bar with them all.

'No man to keep you at home now, Carleen!'

At first she hadn't wanted to go anywhere, scared Joe might come back the very night she was out and be angry to find her missing. But now it's a little more complicated. Carleen knows it would be fun, and she'd appreciate some company for a few hours. But then she remembers she hasn't anything to wear, and with only the one wage coming in, after the bills have been paid there's not much left for beers and bowling.

She can feel her feet throbbing, the dull ache that always starts in her shoulders around that time in the afternoon, and all she wants right then is to be back home. Back home in the house where she keeps everything she has left in her life. Her collection of animal figurines on the shelf above the TV – one of the few things Joe didn't take – her boxes of cereal and microwave dinners kept in neat rows in the cupboard, her clean uniforms hanging side by side in the closet.

Home is where she keeps quiet, keeps her secrets and her temper, keeps herself to herself, keeps wishing things were different. And it's where she keeps wondering why Joe left her for Jenny-Mae.

The diner is where nothing is kept, where everything is temporary, constantly moving, ephemeral, disposable. Brief smiles, insincere greetings, empty coffee cups and ketchup-smeared tables. There is no peace, no calm, only Jodie's high-pitched shouts, Wes's gruff orders, Annie's brittle laugh, and the nausea Carleen feels when her thumb presses into a gloop of egg yoke at the edge of a dirty plate.

Each time the diner door opens it blows something in and sucks something out. Someone new just passing through, someone familiar venting about their bad day; a cold wind, a warm breeze; the scent of stale sweat and sweet perfume;

a bright scarf, an ugly hat; a rucksack to trip over, a new baby to coo over; tears in the corner, peals of laughter by the window; a complaint about the coffee, a compliment to the chef.

When Joe walked out he took everything – didn't leave a single item to prove he had ever been there. But not only did he take his own things, he took some of Carleen's too, and that included most of her clothes. She still has her good jeans – she was wearing them at the mall the morning he took off. But otherwise she has nothing left to wear save for a few old T-shirts, her work uniforms, and the things from the laundry basket. Everything else went with Joe. She reckons he was in a rush, keen to get as far away as he could before she came back home, that he'd simply grabbed all the hangers and thrown everything into his Ford. And she still hasn't told a soul – it feels too strange a thing to say out loud. *My boyfriend left me and took all my clothes.*

As she crosses to the hatch with another pile of plates she spots a folded dollar bill on the floor. Quick as lightning she lets a fork slip to the ground, and as she bends to retrieve it she slides the note down the side of her shoe. As she straightens, she sees the customer at the door. Judging by his suit he won't miss a dollar or two.

When she fishes it out in the restroom her heart skips more than a beat. It's a hundred dollar bill. She folds it neatly, pushes it down her bra as the door swings open.

'You coming out bowling with us tomorrow night, Carleen? Come on girl, you could do to lighten up some. Joe ain't coming back and you know that.'

Carleen looks at Annie, thinks about the pretty red blouse she's seen in the window of Wendy's clothes store on Main Street. 'I might just do that,' she says, smiling.

'Doug will be pleased – you know that too?'

'Get away with you, Annie Rogan, I know no such thing.'

But she smiles again as she opens the door to the grocery store, as she picks up a fresh steak and some good coffee to go with all the week's essentials.

She puts aside a ten dollar bill to pay her mama back a little extra, then checks what she has left. A fifty still waiting to be broken into, a five and a one. As she crosses the road to Wendy's, a woman approaches holding a donation box. She hands Carleen a leaflet about the plight of starving children in some faraway country she's barely aware of. She reaches for the five in her purse and pushes it through the slot before she can think again about the glossy magazine she'd planned to buy from the newsstand.

The blouse is real pretty – it looks more expensive that its twenty dollar tag, and it fits her like a dream. She's lost a good few pounds already since Joe left and she can see she looks the better for it. Though it certainly wasn't planned that way – it's simply that she can't afford the potato chips and beer they used to eat and drink every night in front of the TV.

Wendy nods in approval as Carleen twirls in front of the mirror. She picks up a cherry red hair clip from a display by the counter and passes it to her.

Carleen fastens her hair up properly, tilts her head to one side and takes a final look in the mirror. Satisfied with what she sees, she says she'll take the clip as well, and as Wendy has already turned the sign to 'Closed' she tells her she'll wear the new blouse home to save time. She quickly folds her work shirt and pushes it into her tote, opens her wallet to take out the money. There's a five and a one, but the fifty dollar bill has gone. Without explaining herself, Carleen turns and runs out of the shop, crosses over to the woman with the donation box who's still standing at the corner of Main and Seventh. But when she tells her what's happened, explains her mistake, the woman simply shakes her head.

'Why, how do I know you ain't just saying that? Maybe you seen someone put in a fifty and you're just trying it on? You can't prove a thing.'

'But who would mean to put a goddam fifty in your tin?'

'You'd be surprised, lady.'

The woman looks across at the clothes store, and Carleen turns, sees Wendy watching her from the window – then remembers she's still wearing the red top.

She goes back into the shop, pulling the clip from her hair, and explains to Wendy about the money mix-up as she unbuttons the blouse and pulls her uniform shirt back on.

'Say, you work with Doug, don't you?'

Carleen nods, but Wendy adds nothing further. Then she starts to fold the blouse.

'Here, take it anyway, it looks too good on you for you not to have it. You can pay me when you have the money.'

Carleen hesitates as Wendy pulls a carrier bag from beneath the counter.

'No, I couldn't. Really. But thanks.'

At home she sits in silence, stares at the figurines, doesn't even bother to cook the steak or turn on the TV. When the phone rings, the part of her heart still holding out for Joe starts to flutter like a bird's, but it's only a cold caller selling insurance.

The following afternoon, Doug asks if she's going out with them after work, says he's heard from Annie that she's finally ready to brave their company. She picks up the coffee jug and turns away from him, tells him she has to wash her hair. He laughs and tells her it looks fine.

'Well, to be truthful, I've no spare cash right now for a night out.'

'I'll stand you a few beers – you can pay me back some other time.'

'That's real kind, Doug, but I… I've nothing to wear.'

He laughs. 'You must have something to wear, Carleen? It's only the bowling alley, not the Met Opera!'

'Well I… it's all in the laundry right now. I've nothing at all.'

'Okay, Carleen, you win.' He shakes his head slowly and lifts his hand in defeat as he walks back into the kitchen.

After work she goes straight home and cooks the steak, sits at the table to eat for the first time in weeks. Every evening since Joe left she's wished he would walk back through the door and tell her that Jenny-Mae means nothing to him, admit to making a huge mistake. But tonight, for the first time, she wishes something else.

When the doorbell rings, her heart leaps, but now only the tiniest part of her hopes it will be Joe – the part that can't quite let go. The larger part of her already knows it will be no one important – a pizza delivery guy calling at the wrong house, Minnie from next door wanting to borrow a cup of cooking oil.

'So this is where you keep yourself hidden away? Annie gave me your address, I hope it's okay?'

She stares at him in his best jeans and his blue check shirt, momentarily thrown, then glances down at her creased work blouse and automatically smooths her hair.

Doug hands her a carrier bag from Wendy's store.

'Wendy's my sister. She told me what happened.'

Carleen looks inside the bag, sees the pretty blouse and the red hair clip.

'Call it a gift, or if that makes you feel over-obliged, well then buy me a few beers when you can.'

She nods, smiles, stutters her thanks, but doesn't move away from the door or invite him in.

'What are you waiting for, Carleen? You've kept yourself hidden away here far too long – it's time to move on. Get your glad rags on, or we'll be late.'

Annie and Jodie are already waiting in the bowling alley when the others arrive. Annie waves to Carleen and Doug, then turns and waves to Wes as he walks over from the lockers.

'You're looking good girl – I thought you said you had nothing to wear?' Annie fingers the soft material of Carleen's blouse between her finger and thumb, looks over at Doug and gives them both a knowing look.

'Oh, this old thing? I found it at the back of the wardrobe.' She glances guiltily at Doug, but he winks and walks over to the bar.

He watches her all evening, stands behind her when it's her turn to bowl, whispers advice and encouragement. But each time she turns round he's already gone, chatting to Jodie or Wes. When she sees him at the bar again she goes over to help him carry the drinks back to the table. As she steps away from the counter, a bottle of beer in each hand, she feels his breath in her ear, soft as a feather.

'You seen Joe since he ran out on you, Carleen? You still hoping he's going to walk back through the door? 'Cause

I'm hoping against hope that you ain't.'

She doesn't reply, just keeps staring over at the lanes, watches Annie throw her head back as she laughs at something Wes is saying. Then she half-turns towards him, places one of the bottles back on the counter, rests her fingers on his wrist for a moment.

'No, I'm not hoping that, Doug, not any more. Like you say, I've got to move on.'

When they leave the bowling alley, Doug offers Annie a lift too, and Carleen sits between them, feels his leg pressing against hers on the bench seat. There is something solidly reassuring about the warmth of his thigh, and when his arm brushes against hers she feels the promise of a future waiting, but only if she's brave enough to take it.

When they drop her off, Annie puts her hand on the door frame, leans back through the open window.

'Don't you guys do anything I wouldn't. Remember you've got to work alongside each other come your next shift!'

She blows them a kiss and walks to her door before they can reply. Doug pulls away, grinning, turns the radio up loud, sings along to some song about a guy loving a woman who doesn't even notice he exists.

He stops outside Carleen's house, turns the volume down low, but doesn't switch off the engine.

'I've had a lovely evening, Carleen. Thanks for coming out with me. I know—'

'I've enjoyed it too.' She cuts him off, both scared and hopeful of what he might say. 'It's done me good to get out.'

She reaches for the door handle, pulls it down in slow motion, angry with herself for interrupting, willing him to say something else. When he doesn't, she pushes the door open and steps out into the parking lot. Standing up, she can see over the low fence to her door, can make out something dark on the step, something which looks like a large black bin bag.

'Doug,' she shouts, 'can you tell what that is?' She points towards her entrance porch, and he peers at her for a moment through the windscreen, then opens his door, climbs out and goes over to the building. She sees him kick the bag gently, then bend over, rip the neck open with two hands.

As she walks towards him, he stands back up and holds out a sequinned dress, then a short blue skirt and a crop top.

'Clothes,' he says.

Carleen feels herself blushing, hopes he won't notice in the dark.

'My friend will have left them there,' she says quickly. 'She often leaves a few things with me for the thrift store van.'

He hands her a folded piece of paper with her name on the outside. 'There's a note,' he says.

She takes it from him, strangely unmoved when she sees the writing is Joe's.

Carleen – I took these things by mistake, and I guess you'll be needing them. I'm sorry for all the trouble I caused you.

'Do you want to come in for coffee?' she asks.

'I'd love to – if you're sure? If it ain't too soon?'

Doug follows her inside and drops the sack down in her hallway. Carleen looks at him, then at the ripped bin bag, and figures there isn't room for both of them in her new life. She doesn't like most of those old clothes anyway; Joe chose some of them with her and the rest have seen better days. What was that saying of her mama's – "something in, something out"? She kicks the bag back onto the porch step, throws the note into the waste bin by the hall table and closes the door.

Acknowledgements

I would like to thank Jamie McGarry, Peter Barnfather, and all the team at Valley Press for making this book happen, with particular gratitude to my insightful and thoughtful editor, Teika Bellamy.

Huge thanks also to the talented Suzanne Conboy-Hill for her brilliant cover artwork, and – as always – to Mr L for his ongoing support.

- 'Aleksandr' was Highly Commended in the Fish Short Story Prize and was first published in the *Fish Anthology 2021.*

- 'The Sparrow Steps' won second place in the Writers in Kyoto Annual Writing Competition 2020 and was first published in *Structures of Kyoto* 2021. It was also chosen for the BIFFY50 list of the fifty best UK/Irish flash fictions 2019/2020.

- 'Eating Unobserved' won the Colm Toibin International Short Story Award 2020 and was first published on the Wexford Literary Festival website.

- 'Ten of Hearts' was first published in the Retreat West anthology *Ten Ways the Animals Will Save Us* 2022, and a previous version, 'Cheap Tricks', was broadcast on BBC Radio Leeds in September 2021

- 'An Unfamiliar Landscape' was first published in *Same Same But Different* (Everything with Words) 2021.

- An earlier version of 'The Right Castanets' was first published in the author's flash fiction collection, *Brightly Coloured Horses* (Chapeltown Books) 2018.

- 'A Small Thing to Carry' was inspired by the author's travel piece published in *Traveller* magazine 2014, which won the BGTW New Travel Writer of the Year Award.

- An earlier version of 'In the Time It Takes to Make a Risotto' won the H E Bates Short Story Competition 2021 and was first published on the competition website.

- An earlier version of 'Some Kind of Happy' was first published under the title 'Shooting Stars' in the author's flash collection, *Brightly Coloured Horses* (Chapeltown Books) 2018.